DEAR POPPY

Also by Ronni Arno

Ruby Reinvented

DEAR POPPY

Ronni Arno

ALADDIN M!X
New York London Toronto Sydney New Delhi

ALADDIN M!X
Simon & Schuster Children's Publishing Division
1230 Avenue of the Americas, New York, New York 10020
First Aladdin M!X edition October 2016

Also available in an Aladdin hardcover edition.

Cover designed by Karina Granda
Interior designed by Mike Rosamilia
The text of this book was set in MrsEaves.
Manufactured in the United States of America 0916 OFF
10 9 8 7 6 5 4 3 2 1
Library of Congress Control Number 2016939155
ISBN 978-1-4814-3760-8 (hc)
ISBN 978-1-4814-3759-2 (pbk)
ISBN 978-1-4814-3761-5 (eBook)

For my parents,
who taught me that magic grows
from the seeds of hard work

CHAPTER 1

MY BROTHER IS SMILING SO HARD I THINK HIS CHEEKS are pinned to his ears. This would be fine, of course, if we weren't at my grandfather's funeral.

I elbow him in the ribs.

"What was that for?" He rubs his side.

"You shouldn't look so happy at a funeral," I hiss.

"I'm not *happy*," he says. "I'm just glad Grandad's in a better place."

"And that his truck is still here," I say, teeth clenched.

"Grandad loved that truck, and he wanted me to have it," Troy whispers. "And it's not like he ever drove it once he went into the nursing home."

"It doesn't matter." I cross my arms. "He's dead and it's sad."

My father turns around in the pew in front of us and puts his finger to his lips. "Shhhhh."

I point at Troy with my thumb to show my dad that it was clearly his fault. My dad just shakes his head and turns back around in his seat.

The minister is droning on about how Grandad is reunited with Grandmom and Mom. My stomach sinks a little when I hear Mom's name. I hope and pray that she's up there somewhere, hanging out with her parents, playing Scrabble, looking down on us and smiling. But I don't know. I've asked for a sign every single day since she died five years ago, and I've gotten nothing. Not even one little boo. It's hard to believe that her spirit is still around but never bothered to get in touch.

Finally, we file out of the church. Dad shakes hands with some guy I don't recognize. Like most everyone else in this town, he has a white beard and long white hair—a skinny Santa Claus. Dad looks uncomfortable, shifting from foot to foot, hands fiddling around with his tie. I know he wants to get out of here as soon as possible, but I can't tell if it's because of Skinny Santa Claus, or because he hasn't stepped foot near a church since Mom died.

After the service we follow the hearse to the cemetery. The gray, rainy day makes it look even creepier than it already is. By the time we get to Grandad's grave, I feel like I swallowed a tombstone. We pull up to Grandad's new home—a hole in the ground. At least he's got good neighbors. Grandmom's grave is next to his, and next to hers is Mom's. I haven't been here in a couple of years. Maybe that's why Mom's spirit doesn't visit. She's mad at me for ditching her.

When the casket is ready to go into the ground, Dad squeezes my hand. He looks like he just ate a lemon covered in hot sauce. His eyes keep wandering over to Mom's grave.

Daphne Pickler
Devoted wife and mother
April 3, 1973–March 21, 2011

Her grave site is totally bare. No flowers, no teddy bears, no nothing. I kick myself for not bringing something along with me. Duh. Why didn't I realize that Grandad would be buried with Mom? If Mom wasn't mad before, I'm sure she's furious by now.

I pull my hand out of Dad's and stuff it in my pocket. *He* was supposed to be the one to bring something for Mom. *He* was supposed to know that we were going to be here. *He* was supposed to be the grown-up.

Except that he isn't and he hasn't been. Not since Mom died.

They put Grandad in the ground. I know Troy is right and Grandad hasn't been Grandad for years, but my eyes don't realize this, and tears leak out of them. I quickly wipe them away with the back of my hand. I glance up at Dad, who has his head down and his lips pursed. I feel a twinge of pity for him. Grandad wasn't his father, but he never knew his own father and Grandad was the closest thing he had. Poor Dad, he—

I give myself a mental slap. I am *not* giving Dad a ride on the pity train.

The service ends, and we walk back to the car.

"Can I drive?" Troy eagerly holds out his hands for the keys.

"Not a chance," I pipe in. "I'm not driving with him."

"I have my permit," Troy says. "And anyway, who do you think is going to drive you around when we move?"

What?

"Troy!" Dad shakes his head.

"Oops." Troy slinks to the passenger-side door.

"We're moving?" I ask, after I pick my jaw up off the ground.

Dad turns to look at me. He tries to take my hand again, but I cross my arms instead.

"Poppy, honey." Dad takes a deep breath. "We've moved from tiny apartment to tiny apartment over the last few years. Things haven't exactly been stable."

I snort at the understatement.

"That was your mom's biggest complaint. She always said we needed to go somewhere we could have roots."

I can't believe Dad's trying to use Mom to talk me into this. He hasn't talked about Mom in years.

"Your grandad left us the house." His voice takes on a giddy tone, as if this is the best news ever. "And I think we should move into it and start our lives over. And the house is paid for, so I won't have to be out working so much. We could spend more time together. We could have a real home."

"But here? In a haunted house on hillbilly hill? What about school? What about my friends?"

"The house isn't haunted, Poppy. And don't call the locals hillbillies. Your mom grew up here, you know."

I feel a twinge of guilt pull at my stomach. I didn't mean *Mom* was a hillbilly.

"And you can still see your friends. We can visit each summer." Dad smiles as if I should be doing backflips at the news of seeing my friends once a year.

Ugh. I happen to know for a fact that the house is haunted. Grandmom used to tell me all the time. I know she tried to make it not-scary by saying that the ghosts were friendly, like Casper, but let's face it: How many friendly cartoon ghosts are there in the real world? And based on the people at Grandad's funeral, this place *is* the hillbilly hub of the world.

"And what if I say no?" I cross my arms with finality.

"I'm sorry." Dad sighs. "But the decision's been made. We're going to go over there now and check things out, and then we'll move our things in over the weekend."

I wait for him to say more, but he doesn't. I open my mouth to scream and yell and demand to know why he's all of a sudden deciding to become a parent when he's been nearly absent for the last five years. But instead of words coming out, I just sob. I turn my back on him, open the door, and crawl into the backseat. How can he expect me to switch schools now, in the middle of seventh grade? Isn't there some kind of cruelty-to-children law about that?

But my mouth won't work, except to leak out ugly gurgling sounds. My dad keeps looking at me in the rear-view mirror, but I'm pretty sure his brain turns off at the sound of crying.

My grandparents' old farmhouse sits off a country road, which is miles away from any town center, mall, restaurant, or actual people. Our closest neighbors are a flock of sheep and a herd of cattle. I used to love visiting when I was little. Grandad would always help me pick berries, and let me sit on his lap while he drove the tractor up and down the fields. I was seven the last time I was at the farmhouse. I remember because it was a few months before Mom died and Grandad went into the nursing home. Yep, that was a stellar year.

Dad parks the car next to the garage. Everything looks exactly the same. Grandad had a caretaker living here before he died. But I guess the place is ours now.

The house looks just like I remember it. A giant porch wraps around the building, and the forest-green rocking chairs are in the exact same place they've always been. Mom used to sit me on her lap for hours and we'd rock back and forth, drinking lemonade with fresh mint leaves dropped in. Mom loved mint, and every time I smell it I think of her.

I swallow hard. This place is full of Mom memories, and they come flooding back to me with every whiff of hay and every step in the freshly mowed green grass.

"There she is!" Troy leaps over to Grandad's pickup truck, parked next to the barn. He taps the door gently. "How are you doing, baby? Ready for a new life?"

I roll my eyes. How can Troy be happy about this? Is getting a truck better than switching schools in the middle of the year? Better than leaving the city we've called home since birth? Then I remember how easily Troy can be bought—and distracted. When Mom died, Dad got him a puppy. But Troy got sick of taking care of it after a few months, and we gave it to my cousins who lived in the suburbs. So Dad got him an Xbox instead, and he seemed perfectly content with that.

While Dad and Troy *oooooh* and *aaaaaah* over the truck, I wander over to the barn. Troy and I played hide-and-seek when we were younger, and there was no better hiding spot than the hay bales in the loft. I slide open the barn door, and the memories practically push me over—or maybe it's the stench of horse poop.

The stalls are empty now, but it still smells exactly the same. I climb up the ladder to the loft. The hay bales are still here. I squeeze myself in between two of them and sit there, breathing in the familiar smell of straw. Maybe if I hide in here long enough, I'll be able to miss the rest of seventh grade altogether.

This was a great hiding spot when I was seven, but not so great now that I'm twelve. There's not enough room in between the bales, so I wriggle my butt until each hay bale slides away, giving me more room to sit. I scooch backward until I realize I'm sitting on something hard and pointy.

I quickly stand up and spot the edge of wallboard sticking out. One of the panels must have come loose and fallen down into the hay. I reach my hand out to close it, when I notice a metal box crammed inside. I squeeze my hand into the crack and pull out the box. It's silver, and about the size of a textbook. When I lift it up, I can tell that something's sliding around inside. There's no lock, but it won't open. I pry my fingernails under the lid and pull. The lid pops off, flies through the air, and lands with a *clank* on the barn floor.

Inside are letters. A whole stack of letters, tied up in a rubber band. I flip through the envelopes and notice they all have the same name neatly printed on the outside.

Poppy.

These letters are to me.

I stare at my name. Did someone know we were coming? But why would they leave the letters here, hidden in a stack of hay? And why do they look so *old*?

There are numbers at the top of each envelope. I pull the envelope labeled *#1* out of the rubber band holding the stack together, and flip it over. It's sealed.

Do I open it?

I have to open it. It's not like I'm spying or breaking some sort of federal mail law, or even invading someone's privacy. The letters are addressed to me.

Before I can change my mind, I rip open the top of the yellowed envelope. I gently slide the paper out and carefully unfold it.

April 13, 1985

Dear Poppy,

I wonder about you all the time and I can't wait until you're here! Not much is happening these days—in fact, things are pretty lame. Tammy and Kelly still slip fake love notes into my locker. Of course I know they're fake and I know it's them, but I guess they get their cheap thrills doing those sorts of things. Oh! Brian did smile at me in English class today, so there's a silver lining. I think Tammy noticed, because she glared at me for the rest of the day. Just because she is waiting for him to invite her to the square dance doesn't mean he's not allowed to talk to anybody else, right?

Other than that, my roses are miserable. Maybe they wish you were here too. I think they're wilting. I hope I can save them in time for the 4-H fair, which is eight weeks away. I have to beat Tammy this year.

I just have to. I don't think I can stand another minute of hearing her brag about how great she is. Gag me with a spoon.

I'm going to write to you every single week until the fair. I know you can't get or send mail right now, so I'll save them for you until you can. Just don't read them out of order, and read only one per week. It will be more realistic that way, more like we're in the same room together. Promise? Okay, good!

Until next week.

Love & friendship always & forever,
Daphne

I stare at the letter, holding the paper between my fingers as if it were made of glass. I don't know how this is possible, but somehow it is. Maybe all the years I spent wishing and praying and asking for a sign finally worked.

Because if this isn't a sign, I don't know what is.

This is a letter to me.

And it's from my mother.

CHAPTER 2

MY MOM WAS BORN IN 1973. THIS LETTER WAS written in 1985, which makes her twelve years old. *Exactly the same age that I am now.* What's even creepier? Mom wrote her letter in April. I'm reading her letter in April!

Mom writes that she "wonders" about me and "can't wait" till I'm here. She also knows I "can't get mail right now." Of course I couldn't get mail in 1985. I wasn't even born yet! She must have known I was coming, though. She must have known what my name would be and everything. And she saved these letters for me.

But why?

"Poppy?" Dad's voice echoes through the barn. "You in here?"

"Oh yeah, Dad." I quickly shove the letter back in

the envelope, and something slides out, fluttering to the floor. "Be right there."

I bend down to pick up whatever it was that fell, and when I look at it, I actually gasp. It's a picture of Mom, sitting on a hay bale in this very loft. She's got a cowboy hat on her head, and bright red cowboy boots on her feet. I laugh. I can't believe my mom—my practical, Birkenstock-wearing mom—ever had red cowboy boots.

"Poppy," Dad calls again.

"Coming!" I slide the letter and the photo back into the envelope, hide the box back inside the wall, and close the panel shut. When I get down from the loft, dad is standing there with his eyes closed, taking deep breaths.

"Dad?" I say.

He opens his eyes. "This place sure brings back memories."

I nod.

He shakes his head as if trying to get rid of something that's crawling in his hair. "I, uhhhh, I just wanted to see if you were okay."

"Yeah, Dad. I'm okay."

"I'm sorry we didn't tell you sooner about the move. It's just that it happened so fast. I know you're not happy about it—"

"No, Dad." I cut him off. "It's okay. I'm okay."

"Really?" Dad raises his eyebrows. "Why the sudden change of heart?"

My eyes fly up to the loft. "I guess some things are just meant to be."

We head home, and I spend the long car ride writing back to Mom. Who knows . . . maybe her spirit can read.

Dear Mom,

Thanks so much for writing the letters. I don't know how you knew about me back when you were my age, but I'm glad you did.

You probably know this, but Grandad died and we're moving into the farmhouse. I love the city and don't want to leave my friends, but I'll do anything if it means I get to be closer to you.

I hope you and Grandad and Grandmom are having a good time . . . wherever you are.

Love ya,
Poppy

PS: Nice cowboy boots!

I tuck the letter neatly into my purse. As soon as I get home, I'll find an empty folder to keep them in.

We spend the next few days packing up our apartment. Amanda, my BFF since kindergarten, comes over to help.

"I can't believe you're leaving," she whines. "It's going to be so lame without you."

"Admit it, Mandy," I say. "It's been lame *with* me."

"Well, duh." Amanda rolls her eyes. "It's middle school. But at least we're in it together."

I smile. "You'll be fine. You'll still have Tina and Stevie."

"Ugh." Amanda takes my books off my bookshelf and throws them into a box. "They're totally boy crazy. All they want to do is stalk the boys' soccer team."

I nod. "Yeah, but at least you like the boys' soccer team."

"Aren't you even a little bummed that you're leaving?" Mandy seals a box and looks up at me from her spot on the floor. I plop down next to her.

"Of course." I write BOOKS on the box with my purple sharpie. "But I told you about the letters. I think my mom is trying to tell me something."

Amanda's eyes go wide. "It's so cool that she's

contacting you from the grave. Or, you know, from wherever she is."

"So this is something I have to do." I put my hand on hers. "You understand, right?"

"Of course, Poppy." Amanda squeezes my hand. "It's just that I'll miss you."

"I'll miss you too. But we'll text and video chat. And you can come to the farm to visit any time you want."

Amanda nods, and her eyes get misty.

"Don't you cry, Mandy," I command. "If you cry, I'll cry too."

Amanda waves her hands in front of her face like she's trying to air-dry her eyeballs. "Okay, okay." She takes a deep breath. "Aren't you a little freaked out, though, living in a haunted house on hillbilly hill?"

"Not anymore, now that I know my mom is the one haunting it."

Amanda smiles. "Maybe she couldn't get through to you here in the city; too much pollution between the dimensions."

I shrug. "Maybe."

"Have you met any of the kids who live nearby?"

"No." I seal up a box with packing tape. "I haven't even been there since second grade."

"So are you nervous that you won't know anyone?"

I stop packing and think about the question. Since finding Mom's letters, I haven't even given that any thought. "Not really. I guess I don't care that much."

"Think anyone else will have pink hair?" She glances at my head. Amanda and I both colored the tips of our hair pink last month. The month before was purple.

I laugh. "I really hadn't thought of that."

"I don't know, Poppy." Amanda shakes her head. "It could get pretty boring without any friends."

"I don't need friends." I smile. "I'll have my mom."

We go back to packing up my room until it gets dark. When it's time for her to leave, I give her a big hug and promise to text as soon as I get there.

The next morning, the moving truck arrives, and I'm actually excited to leave. I didn't have time to go back to the barn to grab the letters before heading back to the city, so I had to leave them at the farmhouse. Now, when I should be miserable that I'm leaving Amanda, my home, and the fact that I won't be within a fifty-mile radius of a Starbucks, all I can think about is getting back to those letters. And Mom.

We finally drive back to the farmhouse on a rainy Friday morning. It's a five-hour drive, but it feels like five days. The movers are in the truck behind us, carrying what little furniture we had crammed into our two-bedroom apartment.

Dad tries to talk to me on the car ride, but I tune him out. He's talking about the new school I'll go to, the courses and electives they have, blah, blah, blah. I don't care about any of that stuff. I only care about Mom's letters.

When we pull into the long driveway, I practically leap out of the car while it's still moving.

"Glad to see you're so excited to be here, Poppy," Dad says as he parks the car.

"Yep, can't wait," I call back. I eyeball the barn, and then look at Dad and Troy. I can't let them know about the letters. They're made out to me, not them, and if Dad sees letters from Mom, he'll insist on reading them. Maybe Mom doesn't want Dad to read the letters. After all, she does mention that Brian guy. . . .

I wait until Dad and Troy are busy with the movers to make my mad dash to the barn. It's been exactly one week since I read the first letter. I glance back to the house to be sure nobody's looking, and then I slide open the barn doors and slink inside. I race to the ladder, taking the rungs two at a time, until I'm in the loft. I push the hay bales apart and pull out the metal box containing the letters. It pops open, and I yank the letter marked #2 out of the stack. I rip the top of the envelope, and pull out the piece of paper, which is covered in hand-drawn hearts and stars.

April 20, 1985

Dear Poppy,

You probably think I'm crazy, writing to you like this. I guess I just have to vent sometimes, and it seems more normal to vent to an actual person than to write something in some journal that nobody but me will ever see. I know you'll understand.

I overheard Tammy telling Kelly that her roses are AMAZING. I don't know what's wrong with mine. They were doing really well a month ago, and now they're not. I want to beat Tammy at the fair so badly I can taste it. I think I'll go to the library tomorrow and do some research on how to perk up roses. It's not like I have anything better to do on a Saturday anyway, right? It's not like I'll be doing something fun with my parents. It's springtime, which means farming season, which means they've pretty much forgotten that I exist.

The good part about that is that my mom hasn't noticed that I cut the necks off all my sweatshirts. And when I curl my hair, I look exactly like Alex from Flashdance! Brian even said so when we were at our lockers today. I included a picture so you could see.

Oh, well. At least I have you. Sort of! I just can't wait till you get back from the great beyond and we can have a real talk instead of these silly one-sided letters.

Until next week.

Love & friendship always & forever,
Daphne

I shake the envelope, and a photo tumbles out. I pick it up carefully and hold it up to the light streaming in from the barn window.

Unlike the first photo with the cowboy boots, this one is a close-up of her face. It totally looks like Mom, but it totally doesn't. She still has the same huge smile I remember, but her brown hair, which was short and pixie-like, was ginormous in the picture. It was long and curly, and her bangs stood straight up. I'm guessing her hair made her at least three inches taller than she actually was. Her dark brown eyes, which are highlighted with blue eye shadow, are the exact same color as mine.

I hold both the letter and the picture to my chest, trying to get them as close to my heart as possible. Mom said she couldn't wait until I got back from the "great beyond" so we could really talk. She knew I'd understand how she felt. And I totally do! I feel closer to Mom than I ever have. I don't understand how it's possible that she left these letters here for me, or why, but she did, and that's what counts.

As I hold the letter closer, I feel tears filling my eyes. I haven't missed Mom this much in years. I was only seven when she died. I didn't even know she liked roses. I didn't know her parents ignored her in the spring. I didn't know she looked like Alex from *Flashdance* (I make a mental note to Google that so I know who it is, but I'm guessing she had big hair).

Maybe that's why she wrote me these letters. Maybe she knew that she would die when I was young, and she wanted me to get to know her. My chest feels like it's filled with helium when I realize this. Mom wants me to get to know her now, because I never really got the chance to before.

My thoughts are interrupted by Troy's loud, obnoxious

voice. I wonder if Mom knew that she'd have Troy, too, or if he was an unfortunate accident.

"Hey, Dad, want to take her out for a spin?"

I roll my eyes. All he cares about is that truck.

"Not today, buddy," Dad says. "Let's help get this truck unloaded first. And where's Poppy?"

I know if I don't start helping, he'll come looking for me. I stare at the stack of letters. I'm practically drooling at the thought of opening up letter number three. I want to read on so badly. But then I remember that Mom made me promise to read one a week, so I carefully slide the letter and the photo back into the metal box, and put the box back in its hiding place.

I climb down the ladder and out into the yard. Dad and Troy are lugging boxes from the trunk of our car.

"Where you been, lazybones?" Troy gives me the death stare. I stick my tongue out at him.

"Real mature," he says. As if he's totally mature now just because he knows how to drive. I should remind him that he still tells poop jokes every night over dinner.

I grab a box marked POPPY'S PERSONAL STUFF out of the trunk of Dad's car and lug it upstairs. It feels weird to be moving into my grandparents' house.

"I figured you'd want your regular room," Dad says as he passes me in the kitchen.

I nod. I guess Dad still remembers how much I loved staying in that room when we visited. I clutch the box closer to my chest and climb up the steps. There are four bedrooms upstairs, and I head toward mine. As I reach the end of the hallway, my pace slows down. I know for a fact that this used to be Mom's room when she was a kid. The door is open, and I put the box down on the dresser. Everything's exactly as I remember it. Double bed with a yellow lacy bedspread. A dresser and two matching nightstands painted antique white. An oval rug with tiny red roses covering the floor. I look around for a few seconds, wondering why Mom put the letters in the barn, rather than in here. Unless she left something else for me? I run over to the closet and fling open the door, but it's empty. I check the floor for loose floorboards, but there are none. I open every drawer of both dressers, and even crawl under the bed, but there's nothing. The place is empty.

It doesn't matter. I know Mom is with me. Why else would she have written those letters? She knew I was going to be here. She knew all of this would happen.

I take a deep breath. I just have to trust that she knows what's best for me. She's my Mom, after all.

I dig into one of the boxes until I find a notebook and a pen. Then I write back to Mom.

Dear Mom,

I totally know what you mean about wanting to write to a real person. After you died (that sounds weird), I saw a therapist at school. She said I should keep a diary, but I thought that was a dumb idea, so I never did it.

I'm sorry to hear that your roses weren't doing well. I remember that we had plants around our apartment when I was little, but I didn't realize you liked flowers so much. I guess I was too young to pay attention to that sort of thing.

That Tammy girl sounds like a jerk. When David Trillo was mean to me in first grade, you told me to ignore him, so that would have been my advice to you too.

Can't wait to read your next letter!

Love ya,
Poppy

PS: You had really weird hair when you were 12.

* * *

It takes the movers most of the day to unload the truck and set everything up in the new house. Dad orders pizza for dinner, and we eat it off paper plates.

"School starts Monday," Dad says as he tears the crust off his pizza. Like me, he eats the crust first.

"Yep." I take a sip of lemonade.

"Nervous?" Dad raises his eyebrows.

"A little," I say. Dad hasn't shown much interest in my life since Mom died, so I'm not sure what his motivation is here. Plus, I'm not used to spilling my guts to him, so this feels more like an interview than a real conversation.

"I spoke with the principal last week. They're expecting you."

"Okay." I grab another slice from the pizza box.

"So." My dad grins at me. "Are you excited for Monday?"

"Yes," I answer. And I am. But not because of a new school. I'm excited because another new day means I'm closer to another week, which means I get another letter from Mom. And then I get to thinking . . .

I don't like the fact that Mom's letters are in the barn. Someone else could find them, and anyway, I get the chills when I think of them out there in the cold all alone. I need to bring them inside, where they'll be closer to me.

* * *

At bedtime on Sunday, I set my alarm for six fifteen, a full fifteen minutes earlier than I need to get up in the morning. This will give me time to get to the barn before getting ready for school.

I crawl under the yellow lacy quilt and close my eyes. I don't know how long I'm lying there for, but I can't sleep. I forgot how quiet it is here. No horns, no neighbors, no trains. Since the house is so big, I don't even hear the television my dad's watching. I flip over on my side and put my extra pillow over my head. I'm not sure it's possible to block out the sound of silence, but it's worth a shot.

It must have worked, because the next thing I know, my alarm is blaring. I spring out of bed, tiptoe downstairs, and throw my jacket over my nightgown. I slip on a pair of fuzzy Ugg boots and slowly open the back door. A poof of cold air hits my face as I step outside, and I hold my jacket tightly around me as I run to the barn.

There are goose bumps on my legs as I climb up the loft ladder. I pull the metal box out of the hay and stare at it. Although I want to bring it inside and hide it in my room, where it will be safe and warm and nearby, I'm afraid that will be too tempting. How will I stick to reading one letter per week if the box is so easily accessible? Then again, I can't risk having Dad or Troy finding them. As I stand there shivering, the metal box freezing against my hands, I decide that temptation is the lesser of two evils here. I put the box under one arm and use the other arm to balance myself on the ladder.

I run to the house, and when I swing open the door, my dad is standing right in front of me.

CHAPTER 3

"WHAT ARE YOU DOING, POPPY?"

Dad's hair is sticking straight up and his plaid bathrobe hangs over a T-shirt and sweatpants.

"Oh, uhhhh." I tuck the box underneath my coat and hope he's still too bleary-eyed to notice. "I left something in the car and I just went to get it."

"So early?" He rubs his eyes.

"I didn't want to forget." I do a little bob-and-weave and sneak past him. "Better go get ready for school!"

I run up the steps and into my bedroom. I place the box gently on my nightstand, kick off my boots, and throw my jacket on the floor. It feels like there's a bass drum in my chest, so I take a deep breath to calm myself down. For once, I'm glad Dad is as clueless as he is.

I sit on the edge of my bed and open the box. Letter number three is sitting on top.

I pull it off the stack, and as I'm about to rip the envelope open, I remember what Mom asked. That I read one a week. I sigh. It would be incredibly rude to ignore her rules after all these years of her not having any.

Just as I decide to do the right thing and not open the envelope, I hear Troy's alarm go off in the next room. I glance at my clock—only thirty minutes until the bus comes. I carefully put Mom's letter back, close the lid to the metal box, and hide it in my underwear drawer. That's the good thing about living with fathers and brothers. They never want to look in your underwear drawer.

I tear open the cardboard wardrobe box that's leaning against my closet. As I peek in there, it occurs to me that I have no idea what to wear. It's obviously colder here than in the city, but besides that, I don't know anything else about the area. I guess I should look nice on my first day, so I choose a pair of black skinny jeans, a fuzzy black sweater, and a gray infinity scarf, which I wrap around my neck twice. I add a pair of silver dangling earrings, and flip up my hair so the pink tips are obvious. I coat my eyelashes with a light layer of mascara, and brush some pink shiny lipgloss on my lips.

Ready as I'll ever be, I guess.

I realize that maybe I am a teensy bit nervous when it's time for breakfast. I stare at the cereal swimming in my bowl, but I just can't bring myself to eat it. My stomach feels like it's full of goldfish already. I pour the cereal into the garbage and pack an extra granola bar in my backpack instead.

Troy gobbles down three bowls of cereal. His headphones are on and he's bopping his head and chewing his food to the beat of the music, which I can hear even though I'm sitting across the table. Apparently, the high school bus comes fifteen minutes later than the middle school bus, so Troy's in no rush.

"Poppy?" Dad walks into the kitchen, dressed in overalls and a flannel shirt. "Ready for school?"

My mouth hangs open when I see him. "What are you wearing?"

"Oh, this?" Dad looks down at his outfit and smiles. "Do you like it? It was your grandad's."

"Obviously," I say.

"I thought I'd try it out. Maybe learn a thing or two about farming."

"Farming?" I raise an eyebrow. "You can't even keep the houseplants alive."

"True, but maybe because I never really tried before. I think I'd make a good farmer."

"Dad, you manage restaurants."

"Right," Dad says. "And both restaurants and farmers work with food, so I should be a natural! And now that I've switched to consulting for restaurants rather than being at one every day, I'll have time to learn more about farming."

"Whatever," I mumble. I've never understood my father, so it's nice to know at least some things haven't changed.

"The bus is scheduled to be here in five minutes." Dad taps at his watch. "They pick you up right at the end of the driveway. Isn't that convenient?"

I shrug. I've never taken a bus to school before. I've always lived close enough to walk.

"Remember, when you get there, go straight to the principal's office."

"I know, Dad." I sling my backpack over my shoulder and head for the door.

"Listen." Dad puts his hand on my shoulder and swings me around to face him. "Good luck today."

"Thanks, Dad." I manage a smile, but it's weird to have Dad so in my face like this. Back in the city, he was still sleeping when I went to school and gone at the restaurant when I got home. He usually didn't even get in till the middle of the night, when I was fast asleep. Days would go by where I didn't see him at all.

I trudge down the driveway to wait for the bus, very happy to have my infinity scarf double wrapped. Even though it's the beginning of April and the snow has all melted, it still feels like winter.

I look down the road, but no sign of a bus. I wish I had my phone with me so I could text Amanda, but Dad said the school prohibits personal electronic devices. My eyes do a panoramic sweep, but there's nothing to see. Just fields and meadows, and lots of sky. I wonder how many miles away the nearest living person is.

Just as I'm about to go inside and tell Dad that the bus must have forgotten about me, a rumbling sound echoes in the distance. I look over and sure enough, a big yellow school bus is clamoring down the road. The goldfish in my stomach have turned into dolphins, and I'm pretty sure they're putting on a show in there.

The bus grinds to a stop, and the doors slide open. The bus driver is wearing a gray cap and chewing on a piece of straw. I've never seen anybody actually chew on straw before, and I stare at him for a minute before he speaks.

"Hey, there." He smiles with the straw in between his teeth. "You must be Poppy."

I nod. I wonder how the straw doesn't fall out.

"Welcome aboard." He gestures for me to come in, so I slowly walk up the three steps, which are steeper than they look. My toe gets caught on the last step, and I stumble a bit before my hands reach out and I catch myself on the back of the bus seats.

I look up. The bus is packed, and every single person on it is staring at me.

Someone chuckles from the back of the bus, and a couple of girls giggle with each other, heads huddled together in a seat for two.

I glance past them and look for an empty seat, but there are none.

"Find a seat," the bus driver says, straw still hanging out of his mouth. "I can't move on until you do."

I can feel the heat rising into my cheeks. I'd love to sit down, but there's nowhere to sit. I walk forward on the bus, my eyes quickly moving up and down the rows to find an empty seat.

The only possibility is a two-seater directly in front of the giggling girls. Unfortunately, there's someone already sitting there. Next to him are a backpack and a gym bag, which, I notice, he doesn't move at all as I approach. And then I see why.

He's asleep.

His head is resting on the window next to him. His mouth is slightly open, and his wool hat is halfway covering his eyes.

"Excuse me," I whisper.

The giggling girls laugh even harder.

"Excuse me," I say again.

I can feel the eyes burning me alive. There must be fifty kids on this bus, and they're all looking right at me. All except this one, who still has his eyes closed.

One of the giggling girls kicks the seat in front of her.

"Brody," she yells.

But he doesn't move.

"Brody," the other giggling girl chimes in, and now they're both kicking the back of his seat.

"What?" The boy takes his hat off his head and turns around to look at the girls. They both gesture toward me with their heads, at exactly the same time.

"Oh, sorry," the boy who must be Brody says. He grabs his backpack and puts it on his lap. He rubs his eyes and then looks up at me.

Wow.

Oh, wow.

He has the coolest green eyes I've ever seen. They're like the color of that fake moss that comes in the pots of fake plants (which is the only thing we've ever had in our apartment since Mom died because Dad stinks at taking care of all living things).

"Have you found a seat yet, Poppy?" The bus driver

sounds slightly agitated, and I realize I've been standing here for at least a minute. And it's been at least ten seconds until Brody the Beautiful moved his backpack.

The giggling girls go back to giggling, and I could swear I hear my name as they whisper to each other. I can't be sure, though. I can't hear much over the sound of the pounding in my ears.

I sit down next to Brody, who proceeds to lean his head back against the window. He puts his hat back over his eyes and, I assume, goes back to sleep. The entire bus is still looking at me, but nobody says anything. So I do what I've always done whenever I rode the bus or subway back home. I stare straight ahead, avoid eye contact with anybody, and wait for the ride to be over.

Ten minutes later, we pull into the school parking lot behind several other buses that look exactly the same as mine. Everyone stands, and this wakes Brody up. He stretches, and one of the giggling girls takes that opportunity to reach across and tickle him under the arm.

"Hey, cut it out." Brody puts his arm down, and in doing so, whacks me in the head.

This really makes the giggling girls giggle.

"Oh jeez, I'm sorry," Brody says. And he shoots the girls a nasty look. "Are you okay?"

"I'm fine." I rub my head and don't feel any bumps.

"Really sorry," he says again, and gives me a small smile. He has superwhite teeth.

"It's okay," I say. I look at him for a split second, but look back down at my lap before he notices.

"So." He stands up and grabs his backpack. "Are you new here?"

"Yeah," I say. I stand up also. "Just moved in."

"Oh, into the old Walsh farmhouse?" He's looking right at me now, and I feel my ears heat up.

"Yep, the Walshes are—were—my grandparents."

"Cool," Brody says. Then his lips turn downward. "Oh hey, sorry about your grandpa."

"Thanks," I tell him. "Did you, uhhhhh, did you know my grandad?" He probably wouldn't remember Grandmom, who died when I was only four.

"Sure," Brody says, as if everyone here knows everyone. "But I hadn't seen him in a while. My mom told me your grandpa was in a nursing home or something."

"Yeah, he was." I slowly put my backpack over my shoulder, careful not to hit Brody with it.

"Well, I'm your neighbor." He sticks a hand out. "Brody Fuller."

I shake his hand, and as I do, I feel like I just stuck my finger into an electrical socket. "Poppy Pickler."

"Wait," one of the giggling girls says from behind

me. "Is your name really . . . Poppy Pickler?"

"Yes," I turn around smiling, thinking maybe they knew my grandparents too, and maybe they've heard of me. But they both crack up uncontrollably and put their giggling heads together in a whisperfest.

I'm so busy wondering what's so funny that I don't notice it's our turn to exit the bus. Brody gestures to me, and I turn around to see that everyone behind us is waiting for me to go.

"Oh, thanks," I mutter as I shuffle off the bus. I want to ask him where he lives, since he said he's my neighbor, but I don't get the chance.

The giggling girls are whispering to Brody as we climb down the bus steps, but I can't hear what they're saying. By the time I get off the bus and onto the sidewalk, they're all strolling into the building, laughing with one another.

As I stand there by myself, the reality of this move slaps me in the face. I am all alone, at a brand-new school, in the middle of nowhere, with absolutely no friends.

I take a deep breath and follow the crowd into my new life.

I stop by the principal's office per Dad's orders. The secretary asks me to take a seat in the waiting area across from her desk. There are four chairs there, and one of them is occupied by a girl with a black bandanna on her head.

The secretary pushes the glasses up onto her nose and holds up a sheet of paper. She squints her eyes as she reads. "Poppy Pickler?"

I stand up. "Go ahead in, hon." She motions to the door on my right.

"What?" Bandanna Girl jumps out of her chair. "I was here first."

"Relax." The secretary looks down at her computer as she talks. "It will be your turn soon enough."

Bandanna Girl slumps back in her chair, and I scurry into the principal's office before she can tackle me.

"Ahhhhhh, Ms. Pickler." The principal motions for me to sit down in the seat across from his. "Welcome to East Valley Middle School. I'm Mr. Russo."

"Nice to meet you," I say. Mr. Russo is dressed in black jeans, a white button-down shirt, and a silver skinny tie, which matches his silver hair perfectly. I wonder if he planned it that way.

"So you're new here?" He flips through a folder with my name on it.

"Yep, we just moved to the area."

"Great, great," he says, still reading what looks like my grades from last year. "It looks like we've got you set up in all of your classes. You'll just need to pick an elective."

"Okay." I nod.

"Let's see." Mr. Russo picks another folder off his desk. "This semester's electives for seventh grade are chorus, Line Dancing, or Intro to Agriculture."

"Ummmm," I mutter. "I can't sing, and I have no idea what the other two electives are."

Mr. Russo chuckles. "You city kids. You're missing out! Line Dancing is a lot of fun. The class learns choreographed dances that are performed in a line."

I cringe as I picture myself bumping into the other students, who are decked out in their finest cowboy boots, as they all turn left and I turn right. "What's Intro to Agriculture?"

"That class will teach you about plants and—"

"Plants?" I remember the roses in Mom's letter. I'm sure this is the class I'm supposed to take. "I'll take that one."

"Don't you want to hear more about it?" Mr. Russo raises his eyebrows. "It's one of the more intense electives."

"That's the one I'd like."

"Okay, then." Mr. Russo marks something on the paper. "Intro to Agriculture it is. Be sure to hold on to your schedule for a while. We have A and B weeks here, so it can get a little confusing."

Just as Mr. Russo hands me my final schedule, there's a knock on the door. A blond girl peeks her head in, and I recognize her as one of the giggling girls behind me on the bus.

"Ahhhh, Ms. Woodruff." Mr. Russo stands up. "You're right on time."

"Hello, Principal Russo," Giggling Girl says, and she extends her hand to shake his.

Who shakes the principal's hand?

"Kathryn Woodruff, this is Poppy Pickler," Mr. Russo says.

"It's so nice to meet you, Poppy." Giggling Girl, whose name is apparently Kathryn, extends her hand to me.

I reach out and take it, and she shakes it so hard I think my arm might dislocate from my shoulder.

"Nice to meet you too." I wonder if I should say anything about the fact that she sat behind me on the bus this morning, but decide against it.

"Kathryn is going to be your tour guide this week," Mr. Russo says. "She'll show you around, introduce you to the other students, and make sure you get to all of your classes on time."

"That's great." I give Kathryn a slight smile. "Thank you."

"Oh, it's my pleasure." Kathryn practically bounces up and down. "I'm so happy to welcome you to EVMS!"

My smile gets wider. Kathryn's enthusiasm pours off her, and some of it must land on me, because I'm suddenly feeling genuinely excited to be here. Not only will I have my mom watching over me, but I'll have new friends, too.

Mr. Russo glances at the clock. "You girls had better get going. Homeroom starts in five minutes."

Kathryn puts her hand on my arm. "You're going to *love* Mrs. Simmons, our homeroom teacher. She is so awesome."

"Oh, good," I say. "Are you in all of my classes?"

"Can I see your schedule?" Kathryn tilts her head and holds out her hand. I give her the paper Mr. Russo just gave me. Her eyes scan the page, and she flashes me a smile so bright I actually have to look away for a minute. It's like there's a candle behind her front teeth. "This is amazing! We have the exact same schedule."

My shoulders must drop three inches. I'm instantly relieved to know that I'll have a friendly face in all of my classes.

"Come on." Kathryn links her arm through mine. "I'll tell you everything you need to know about EVMS."

Kathryn and I walk arm in arm out of Mr. Russo's office. Bandanna Girl glares at us as we saunter past. I ignore her.

"So," I say just as the office door closes and we're out in the hallway. "What do I need to know about EVMS?"

"One very important thing." Kathryn pulls her arm out of mine and looks straight at me, her eyes turning from delightful to deadly. "Stay away from Brody Fuller. Or you'll wish you never left that stuck-up city of yours."

CHAPTER 4

SHE TURNS ON HER HEELS, AND MY BRAIN IS TOO stunned to get the message to my feet that I'm supposed to follow her.

Kathryn looks over her shoulder. "Well," she huffs. "Are you coming?"

I adjust my backpack and weave through the sea of unfamiliar faces until I'm directly behind her, her blond ponytail swishing in my face.

She stops to talk with a few other girls, who all huddle around her like she's the star quarterback about to make the winning play. I stand on the outside of the huddle, alone. Kathryn doesn't introduce me to anyone. She just talks and laughs like I'm not even there. Finally, someone notices.

"Hi," a girl with dark curly hair says. "Can I help you find something? You look lost."

But before I can answer, Kathryn chimes in. "Oh, don't worry about her. She's nobody."

The girl with dark curly hair shrugs, and they all go back into their huddle.

She's nobody.

I squeeze my eyes shut so no tears leak out.

I will not cry. I will not cry. I will not cry.

I remind myself that I'm not here to make friends. I'm here to be close to Mom. I have to remind myself a few times, and when I'm satisfied that I actually believe it, I open my eyes. Kathryn is walking again, and I step up my pace so I can follow her.

She turns into a classroom, which is already packed with students. Some are talking in bunches at their desks; some are flinging crumpled-up paper balls at each other. Kathryn goes directly to a group of four girls—I recognize the other giggling girl from the bus—and another huddle forms. They're whispering, and all four girls turn to look at me at the same time. I'm just standing in the doorway, holding tightly on to my backpack, mostly because I realize I have no idea what to do with my hands. What do my hands normally do? I suddenly can't remember.

A teacher walks in and puts a huge cup of steaming

coffee on her desk. Before I know it, Kathryn's at my side, her arm once again linked in mine.

"Mrs. Simmons," Kathryn calls as she walks me over to the teacher. "This is Poppy Pickler, our new student." Kathryn is beaming at me as if I'm a gold medal she won at the Fake Friendship Olympics.

"Oh, Poppy!" Mrs. Simmons clasps her hands together. "Welcome! We've been expecting you."

"Thank you," I mumble. My brain is still reeling from dealing with the multiple personalities of Kathryn.

"Mr. Russo has asked me to show Poppy around." Kathryn flashes me a smile.

"Wonderful," Mrs. Simmons says. "She couldn't ask for a better host."

"And I couldn't ask for a better new friend," Kathryn says.

Excuse me?

"Class, can I have your attention, please?" Mrs. Simmons claps her hands three times. "I'd like to introduce our new student to you. This is Poppy."

I stare out at the faces, all smiles except for the four girls Kathryn was talking to earlier. They just whisper to each other, stopping long enough to give me the death stare.

"Poppy is lucky enough to have Kathryn as her tour

guide," Mrs. Simmons continues. "But I expect all of you to pitch in and make her feel welcome."

The class nods in unison.

"Okay, class, take your seats," Mrs. Simmons says.

Kathryn unlinks her arm with mine, and bops over to her desk. I'm standing in the front of the classroom, still clutching my backpack.

"I believe there's an empty seat right there, Poppy." Mrs. Simmons points to a desk in the third row. "You're welcome to it."

I slide into the chair and put my backpack on the floor next to me. Just like on the bus this morning, I stare straight ahead. Which is why I don't see a boy running down the aisle and past my desk. He trips over my backpack and winds up sprawled facedown on the floor.

"Thomas, are you okay?" Mrs. Simmons comes running over, her heels *click-clack*ing on the linoleum floor.

"What the—" Thomas jumps to his feet. "What's that backpack doing in the middle of the aisle?"

My ears are burning, and I'm sure my face won't be far behind. "I'm so sorry." I kick the backpack underneath my desk. "I—I—I didn't know where to put it, and—"

"Didn't they give you a locker, Poppy?" Mrs. Simmons and Thomas are both looking down at me.

"I, uhhhh, I don't know." I'm not the kind of person

who's usually at a loss for words, but with all these unfamiliar faces staring at me, my mouth is forgetting how to operate.

"Oh my goodness!" Kathryn stands up from her chair a few rows over and bounces to my desk. "I did give you your locker number and combination, didn't I?"

The fabulous four giggle.

"I don't think so," I mutter.

"Really?" Kathryn purses her lips. "I'm almost positive I did."

Before I could tell her that I'm positive she didn't, Mrs. Simmons pipes in. "Be sure to do that again after homeroom, Kathryn. Poppy has a lot to take in, so she might need some reminders."

"Of course, Mrs. Simmons." Kathryn nods her head, and her ponytail does a little dance behind her. "I hope you're okay, Thomas."

Thomas looks at her and grins. "Yeah, I'm fine."

"Thank goodness for that." Kathryn touches him on the elbow, and Thomas's face turns bright red.

"All's well that ends well," Mrs. Simmons said. "Now please get to your desks for roll call."

I'm so angry about Kathryn's locker lie that I'm surprised to hear my name from the desk next to mine.

"Hey, Poppy."

I turn, and find Brody Fuller and his moss-green eyes sitting there. Right next to me.

"Hi, Brody." I smile, and then remember Kathryn's threat. I glance back at her, and sure enough, she's zapping me with her laser-beam eyes.

I pull my schedule out of my backpack and pretend to study it.

"What do you have next?" Brody whispers.

"Science." I say it so quietly that I barely hear it. I don't need any more trouble from Kathryn.

"Cool," Brody says. "Me too."

I smile, but I don't turn my head to look at him. I can feel Kathryn's eyes burning holes into the back of my skull.

Mrs. Simmons calls each name alphabetically. Everyone's present, until she gets to the *F*s.

"Britt Fuller?" Mrs. Simmons glances up from her attendance sheet. "Brody, is your sister in today?" All eyes turn to Brody.

Brody shrugs. "I have no idea. I took the bus this morning, but she wasn't on it."

Mrs. Simmons lets out a loud sigh. "Do you know if she's sick?"

"I'm not sure what's wrong with her," Brody says under his breath.

"Pardon?" Mrs. Simmons says.

"I don't know. I don't think so," Brody answers.

"Okay, then, I'll mark her absent for now." Mrs. Simmons continues with the roll call. Just as she's finishing up, someone swings open the classroom door so hard that it slams into the wall with a *thud*. I snap my head up to look, as does everyone else in the class.

It's Bandanna Girl. And she looks mad.

"Ahhhh, Miss Fuller. So nice of you to join us."

Miss *Fuller*? Is Bandanna Girl Brody Fuller's *sister*? I take a good look at her. It's hard to see beyond the bandanna, ripped jeans with chains coming out of the pocket, and black Doc Martens, but when I really study her face, I can see it. Their hair is the same cocoa color of brown, and although the bandanna practically covers her eyes, I can see that they're the same awesome color as her brother's.

Bandanna Girl stands in the doorway, scanning the classroom. Her eyes stop on me.

"It's her fault!" Bandanna Girl points a finger at me. Her nails are painted black. "It's that new girl's fault that I'm late."

All eyes go from Bandanna Girl to me, and I wish I could just melt into my chair.

"Now, Britt," Mrs. Simmons says. "Poppy's new here. I'm sure she didn't do anything to delay your arrival."

"She cut me at Mr. Russo's office," Britt says, still pointing at me.

"I'm sure she didn't mean to. Now please take your seat."

Britt collapses into her chair, but she doesn't take her evil eyes off me.

I've been here for fifteen minutes, and already two people hate me.

Mom better have a good reason for putting me through this.

CHAPTER 5

THE BELL RINGS, AND KATHRYN IS AT MY DESK, ALL unicorns and butterflies.

"Ready for science?" She looks past me at Mrs. Simmons, who smiles at her gratefully.

"Hey, sorry about my sister." Brody stands up and stretches.

I glance up at his sideways grin. "Oh, it's okay. She's not that bad," I lie.

Brody laughs. "That's only because you don't have to live with her."

I chuckle, and Kathryn clears her throat. "We need to set up your locker."

"Oh yeah, thanks." I pick up my backpack, and follow Kathryn out into the hallway. She looks toward Mrs.

Simmons, who's busy erasing the whiteboard, and then sneers at me.

I try not to look back at her, and silently follow her toward the lockers.

"Which locker did you get?" Brody asks.

I'm about to answer that I don't know—Kathryn never told me—when Kathryn answers for me.

"She has two fifty-six."

"Cool!" Brody puts his hand up for a high five. "I'm at two fifty-four."

I tap Brody's hand for a quick high five. Kathryn picks up her pace and stomps toward a row of lockers. I can see the steam coming out of her ears, but what was I supposed to do? I couldn't just leave Brody hanging.

We stop at locker 256, and Kathryn shoves a crumpled-up piece of paper in my hand. "Here's your combination."

I stare at the wad of paper. It's still hot from Kathryn's fist. I think I may even see fingernail dents in it.

"Thanks." I smile at her, but she just glares at me.

"Let's go, Brody." Kathryn touches him on the arm. "We don't want to be late for class."

"Shouldn't we wait for Poppy? Aren't you her guide or something?" Brody leans against the locker next to mine.

Kathryn's jaw is clenched so tightly that I'm expecting

her perfect teeth to come tumbling out of her mouth at any second. "Fine," she says. "But she'd better hurry up. Class is starting soon."

I unwad the ball of paper and unlock my locker. I hang up my jacket and backpack and pull out a notebook and pen to take with me to my next class.

Kathryn sighs. "Are you ready yet?"

I close the locker door and nod. She mumbles something under her breath, and I follow her down the hall. Brody stops to talk to some guy on the way, which leaves me alone with Kathryn.

"Just so you know, you're a total outsider here," Kathryn says, without slowing down her pace. "Look around. Nobody here wears all black, for one thing."

I look down at my outfit. At home, black is the go-to color. Everyone wears black. Black matches everything.

"And that hair," Kathryn continues. "What's with the pink ends? Are you in some kind of cult or something?"

My fingers fly to the tips of my hair. A cult? What kind of cult has members with pink hair tips?

"You're obviously a freak, and we don't need any more freaks at EVMS."

"You don't know anything about me." I blurt it out without thinking first.

Kathryn stops walking. She puts her hands on her hips

and looks me up and down. "I know everything I need to know. Brody's got enough on his plate, dealing with his freak sister. He doesn't need another weirdo in his life."

"Look." I take a deep breath. I don't want any trouble from Kathryn, but I can't let her walk all over me either. "I don't know you, and you don't know me. But we both have to go to school here. So let's just agree to coexist peacefully."

Kathryn smiles. "Fine. As long as you don't talk to Brody Fuller."

"What if he talks to me first? You want me to totally ignore him?"

"Yes." Kathryn gives me one crisp nod. "That's exactly what I want you to do."

Just then, Brody catches up to us. "What's up?" He slaps me on the back, and I cringe.

"Oh, I was just helping Poppy navigate the scene around here. You know, letting her know who she should hang out with, and who's trouble."

"Ahhhh, that's easy." Brody smiles and I bite my lip—hard—so I don't smile back. "Hang out with me and you'll be fine."

"Oh, Brody." Kathryn flips her ponytail. It comes centimeters from whacking me in the face. That thing should be registered as a lethal weapon. "You're so funny."

Brody laughs, and he and Kathryn start walking. I follow, keeping my distance a few steps behind them.

They stop to chat with a few kids along the way. Brody introduces me to everyone who talks to us, but Kathryn acts like I'm not even there. That's fine with me. If she's ignoring me, at least she's not making my life miserable.

Once we walk into the science classroom, Kathryn's metamorphosis begins. She links her arm in mine, and guides me toward the teacher's desk.

"Good morning, Mr. Walker," Kathryn says. "This is Poppy Pickler. She's our new student."

Mr. Walker extends his hand, and I shake it. Kathryn's glued to my side, her fake smile blinding me once again.

"Great to meet you, Poppy. Have you studied plant anatomy yet?"

"No." I shake my head. "We didn't do that at my old school."

"Excellent!" Mr. Walker beams. "Then you're sure to have some fun!"

Mr. Walker points me to a seat in the first row, which, thankfully, is on the other side of the room from both Brody and Kathryn. Kathryn's surrounded by a group of girls, and just like in homeroom, she's whispering to them frantically. Every once in a while one of them turns to look at me. Suddenly, I find my own fingernails very interesting.

The bell rings, and Mr. Walker closes the door. "Okay, gang, settle down."

The class gets quiet, and Mr. Walker continues. "Today, we're going to learn about plant genealogy."

The class collectively groans. Mr. Walker walks to the front of his desk and sits on top of it. "Come on, guys, this will be fun. We'll—"

The classroom door swings open, and Britt Fuller stomps in. I can hear Kathryn and her gaggle of girls whispering in the back.

"As I was saying," Mr. Walker continues, a bit louder now, "we're going to learn about how plants are related to each other."

Britt throws her books on top of her desk, which happens to be right next to mine. I keep my eyes glued to Mr. Walker, afraid to look at her.

Thankfully, Mr. Walker doesn't stop to take a breath. He goes on and on about plant DNA, using words I've never heard before.

"Okay, gang." Mr. Walker glances at his watch. "We have an assignment. But we're going to do it in a way that will be fun for you."

"Does that mean you're just going to give us all the answers?" a boy in the back row asks. "Because that's the only way to make plant DNA fun."

Everyone laughs, and even Mr. Walker chuckles. "Very funny. No, I have an even better idea. You're going to all do a family tree, but instead of a family tree, it's going to be a plant tree. Get it? A plant tree?"

Another collective groan.

"But not to worry." Mr. Walker stands up. "I won't leave you to your own devices completely. I'm going to partner you up so you can work together."

Kathryn's hand shoots up. "Can we pick our own partners?"

"Sure," Mr. Walker says. And at that, kids all turn to each other, the room filling with chatter.

Mr. Walker must notice that I'm sitting alone in silence, so he walks over to my desk. "What do you think, Poppy? Is this all new to you?"

"Yes." I nod. "We haven't done any of this at my old school."

"Great." Mr. Walker claps his hands together, and I sigh with relief, thinking that he'll probably excuse me from this project. "Then why don't you and Britt work together?"

I open my mouth to protest, but Britt beats me to it.

"You want me to work with *her*?" Britt's lips pull back, and she bares her teeth at me.

"I think you'll be a good pair," Mr. Walker says, and he walks back to his desk smiling.

Britt leans back in her chair so the front two legs are off the floor. She crosses her arms and glares at me.

"So." I look around the room. All the other pairs are chattering away and taking notes. "How should we start?"

Britt reaches over and grabs the textbook on my desk. She flips through it until she finds the page she's looking for, and throws it back at me.

"Read this chapter. You can't help if you don't know what you're doing, and there's no way I'm going to do the work for you."

She then opens her own notebook and starts writing.

As if this day couldn't get any worse.

CHAPTER 6

THE BELL RINGS, AND AS IF ON CUE, KATHRYN'S AT MY side, playing the part of perfect hostess, at least while we're in earshot of the teachers.

"Ready for math?"

I don't even bother smiling. I pick up my notebook, pen, and new copy of *DISCOVERING SCIENCE: GRADE 7*, and follow her out of the classroom.

Brody walks up behind us, tapping both of us on the shoulder, then looking away like he didn't do it.

Kathryn swats at his hand. "Hi, partner."

Brody groans. "That was a hard project."

"It was fun." Kathryn grins, and then talks louder—to be sure I can hear her above the hallway din. "And since you worked with me, of course we'll get a good grade."

"Yeah," Brody says. "Thanks for snagging me back there. I was afraid I'd have to work with Thomas, and we'd both totally fail."

Kathryn juts her chin out, making her face pointier than it already is. "I'm happy to help."

"Did you find a partner?" Brody asks me.

"Mr. Walker partnered me up with your sister."

Kathryn laughs hysterically. She has to stop walking because she's doubled over. I guess it's okay if I talk to Brody, as long as I say things like that.

Brody looks at Kathryn and I see a flash of something across his eyes. Anger? I can't tell, because in a second it's gone. He turns back to me and shrugs. "Well, she's tough to work with, but Britt knows her stuff. I'm sure you'll get a good grade."

I want to tell him that although I know nothing about DNA, it's not the grade I'm worried about—it's that Britt will tear my flesh off my bones and then make a soup out of my eyeballs. But I don't say that. I don't say it because I'm not allowed to talk to Brody Fuller if I want to get through this school year unscathed. I remind myself that I don't need friends, but I also don't need enemies, and that I just have to stay under the radar until I learn what Mom has in store for me.

Math class at EVMS is like math class everywhere else.

There are numbers, and more numbers. Kathryn happily introduces me to my math teacher, and then promptly ignores me until the bell rings and the teacher is watching. We go through the same drill in social studies.

After social studies is lunch, and once we're not in front of any faculty, Kathryn ditches me and heads for the cafeteria with a group of girls in matching ponytails. There must be a dozen of them, and they all look identical. Same swishy ponytail, same pair of jeans folded up at the bottom, same knit sweaters, and same pearl earrings. I wonder if they call each other every morning, or if everyone just wears the same thing every day.

I buy a grilled cheese sandwich and a bag of chips, and find an empty table—on the opposite side of the cafeteria from Kathryn.

I'm about to bite into my sandwich when I hear someone breathing loudly behind me. I turn around and find Britt standing over me.

"You're at my table."

"Oh." My sandwich suddenly looks unappetizing, and I wrap it up and scootch my chair back. "Sorry, I didn't know."

I'm about to leave when Britt sits down. "Why aren't you sitting with your friends, anyway?"

"My friends?"

"Yeah." Britt motions across the cafeteria. "Kathryn and her Crappy Cronies?"

"They're not my friends." I look down at my wrapped-up sandwich.

"Seriously? She's been glued to you all day."

"Only because she wants to impress the teachers. As soon as we're out of their sight she goes back to ignoring me. Or threatening my life."

Britt laughs, and it's not the kind of laugh I'd expect from her. It's sweet and light, and when I glance up at her face, I see that not only does she have her brother's eyes, she also has his smile.

Just hearing her laugh makes me laugh too.

"I thought for sure she'd snag you for part of her gang. You've got the look."

"The look?" I raise an eyebrow at her.

"Yeah, you know, the pretty-girl thing." She pulls a lemonade out of a paper bag.

"Ummmm. Thank you?" I'm not sure if this is a compliment or not. "But apparently, I have the wrong hair."

"Well, obviously." Britt points to my pink tips. "But hair can be changed. That's what Kathryn does. She hand-selects the girls she deems worthy of her little clique, and before you know it, they slowly morph into one collective person."

"That's kind of creepy," I say.

"Yeah." Brit opens her lemonade and takes a sip. "I just figured you were one of them."

"Definitely not."

We sit in silence for a minute. We actually had a kinda sorta conversation, and now I'm not sure if I should be leaving or not.

"You can sit here if you want," Britt says, answering my unspoken question.

"Okay, thanks." I unwrap my sandwich again, and realize that I'm absolutely starving.

"I'm sorry about science class," she says between sips of lemonade. "I was a jerk to you."

"Yeah, you were." I smile so she knows I'm over it.

"Kathryn and her friends are kind of awful."

"Yeah." I take a bite of my sandwich. "I kind of got that."

"So you moved into the Walsh farmhouse?" Britt pulls a peanut butter and jelly sandwich out of a Ziploc bag.

"Yeah." I take another bite of grilled cheese. "How did you know?"

"It's a small town," she says.

She opens her mouth like she wants to say something, but instead she tears the crust off her sandwich and pops it into her mouth.

"I'm sorry about your grandpa," she says after a few seconds of silence.

"Oh, thanks," I say.

"He was a really nice man."

"Did you know him?" I ask.

"Yeah." Britt takes a bite of her now-crustless pb&j. "I mean, we haven't seen him in a while, not since I was little, but my mom used to buy lots of produce from him. He had the best berries."

"I know, right?" My mouth waters just thinking about them.

"Anyway, I was real sorry when I heard."

"Well, thanks," I say, and tear open my bag of chips. "So you're my neighbor? I didn't even know there were any other houses nearby."

"My house is only about a mile up the road," Britt says. "Not far."

"A mile isn't far?" I crunch on a potato chip. "Where I used to live, a mile would put me in a completely different neighborhood."

"Really?" Britt's eyes go wide. "That's so weird."

"Were you on the bus this morning?"

Britt rolls her eyes. "I hate the bus. I ride my bike when it's nice enough out."

"That's a long ride." I take another potato chip out of the bag.

"Nah, only a few miles. It's better than the stupid bus."

I nod. The bus ride was pretty awful, but I'm not sure I could ride my bike up and down all those hills.

"So, um, anyway." Britt puts the cap on her lemonade bottle and shakes it. "Sorry about this morning, too. I mean, at the principal's office."

"Oh, no worries." I wave my hand in front of my face. "You *were* there first."

"I was there to tell Mr. Russo that someone's been messing with my locker, and I'm pretty sure it's Kathryn and the Cronies."

"What did he say?" I put my grilled cheese down and move my chair closer to hers.

"He didn't believe me, of course." She leans back in her chair, so that the front two legs are off the floor. "You see how sweet Kathryn acts in front of the teachers."

I snort. "I don't know how any of them even fall for it."

"Please," Britt says. "She's been like that since kindergarten. She used to put glue in my crayon box."

"That's so wrong." I shake my head.

"What's wrong is that she gets away with it," Britt says. "But her mom is some bigwig on the school board, so the teachers never bother to listen to me."

Just as I'm about to tell her how unfair that is, I notice that one of the ponytailed Cronies is walking our way. I'm pretty sure she's the girl who was sitting next to Kathryn on the bus this morning. I'm about to say something to Britt when the girl breaks into a jog, swerves just as she gets to our table, and knocks into the back legs of Britt's chair. Since Britt was balancing on only the back legs, the chair crashes to the ground, taking Britt down with it.

"Omigod!" the Crony cries, covering her mouth with her hand. "I'm so sorry." Then she looks back at Kathryn and crew, and they're all cracking up.

By now, the entire seventh grade is watching.

Britt jumps up, eyes blazing. "You did that on purpose, Emily!"

"You can't prove anything," Emily hisses. "And anyway, you're not supposed to tilt your chair back like that. Don't all the teachers tell you that?"

"You little . . ." Britt's hand clenches into a fist, and she pulls her arm back as if she's going to punch Emily square in the nose, which she totally deserves. Emily screams, and just as Britt's about to let her arm fly, Brody runs up behind her and grabs her hand.

"Don't do it," he whispers.

Britt turns around to face him, her cheeks bright red. "Did you see what that little brat did to me?"

Brody looks up at Emily, who's still got her hand up to her mouth, and is cowering behind a chair.

"It was an accident, Brody," Emily cries. "I swear. And now she's going to kill me!"

"You're right I'm going to—" Britt says through clenched teeth.

"Nobody's going to kill anyone." Brody stares at Britt and raises his eyebrows. "All right?"

Britt pulls her hand out of Brody's and picks up her chair. "Just get out of my sight," she snaps at Emily.

Emily runs back to her table, her ponytail bopping up and down. Kathryn and the Cronies are laughing so hard they're crying, but I think Emily may actually *be* crying. I'm not sure what would have happened to her if Brody didn't step in.

Once everyone realizes the fight isn't going to happen, they go back to their food and lunchtime chatter. Brody pulls up a chair next to Britt, and sits on it backward.

"Are you okay?" Brody whispers.

"Did you see what happened? She did that on purpose!" Britt's hand is shaking.

"You don't know that." Brody shakes his head.

Britt turns to look at me, and I nod. "She did, Brody. I saw the whole thing."

Brody takes a deep breath and holds it. "Well, it doesn't matter. You've got to stay in control."

"That's easy for you to say." Britt is speaking very

slowly, like she's carefully choosing every word. "They don't go after you."

"I'll talk to them," Brody says.

"Sure you will," Britt mutters.

"Just . . ." Brody leans in closer to Britt. "Just think of Mom, okay? You getting kicked out of school would destroy her."

Britt closes her eyes, and leans back in her chair. Like before, the front two legs are off the ground. Brody pushes the chair back down. "And don't do that. It's dangerous."

He then stands up, shakes his head, and goes back to his own table.

Within seconds, Kathryn is at Brody's side, whispering in his ear. He's nodding, and she's smiling.

"She makes me sick." Britt is staring at them too.

"Maybe he's talking to her about it," I say.

Britt shakes her head. "He's not. This might be your first day here, but this stuff happens day after day, and has ever since we were little kids. Nothing's ever going to change. My popular brother hates conflict."

"He seems really nice," I say, more to myself than to her.

"Oh, he's a peach." She crumples up her paper bag and squeezes it until it's the size of a Ping-Pong ball. "As long as you're happy and popular. If you're not, you may as well not exist."

I look over to Kathryn's table, where the Cronies are all laughing and pointing—at Britt and me.

"So enjoy him while you can." Britt follows my gaze. "Because once they get through with destroying your reputation, you'll disappear off Brody's radar."

Even though she didn't say it to be mean, her words sting. Brody is one of the few people at this school who is actually nice to me. I mean, yeah, he's really cute, too, but I don't even care about that.

Much.

I glance at the clock on the wall. Twelve twenty. Only two hours and ten minutes until dismissal, eight and a half hours until bed, and then it will be tomorrow. Then, only five more days until a new letter.

I really hope Mom starts explaining things soon.

CHAPTER 7

LIKE CLOCKWORK, KATHRYN REAPPEARS AT MY SIDE to walk me into Spanish, and then does the same thing when it's time for language arts and music.

When the final bell rings, I go to my locker to gather the books I need for homework. I put in the combination, but the locker doesn't open. I turn the dial again—twenty-seven, thirty-two, five—and pull on the handle.

Nothing.

Brody looks over from his locker. "Having trouble?"

I'm sure my face is bright red, either from straining so hard to open my locker or from utter embarrassment that Brody noticed.

I step back. "It's stuck."

"Let me try." Brody closes his own locker, and I step

aside. He starts turning the dial. "What's the combination?"

I look around. Should I be giving strangers the combination to my locker? Even though Brody is my neighbor and he has very nice eyes, he still sort of counts as a stranger. I mean, I've only known him for one day.

Then again, if I don't give him my combination, I'll never get my locker open. I take a deep breath and say the combination as quietly as I can.

He spins the dial—twenty-seven, thirty-two, five—and gets the same result I got. He tries again, but the locker still doesn't open.

Kathryn saunters over with Emily. She sticks her lower lip out. "Oh no. Locker problems?"

"Poppy's locker is stuck." Brody spins the dial again.

"That's too bad, Brody, but you're going to miss the bus if you don't get moving." Kathryn and Emily glare at me in unison.

"Go on, Brody," I say. "I'll figure it out."

"But what if you miss the bus?"

"I can always call my dad for a ride."

"Are you sure?" Brody looks at me and my stomach does a little flip-flop. Kathryn and Emily are tapping their feet, their arms crossed. I notice they have matching silver nail polish. Of course.

"I'm sure. Thanks anyway." I manage to give him a smile after Kathryn and Emily decide it's safe to head out to the bus.

Brody puts his gray hat on and waves at me. "Good luck! Hopefully I'll see you on the bus."

I wave back, then try my locker one more time.

Once again, it doesn't open.

I make my way back through the crowd of students headed for the exit. After a few wrong turns, I find the main office and step inside.

"Can I help you?" The secretary doesn't look up from her computer.

"Yes, my locker isn't working."

"Your locker number and name?" She continues to stare at her computer screen, typing a million words a minute.

"Two fifty-six. Poppy Pickler." I shove my hands in the pockets of my pants.

The secretary snaps her head up. "Oh, Poppy. It's still not working, hon?"

"Still?" I'm not sure what she means by that.

"Kathryn was in here earlier and told us that you were having a problem, so we changed the combination." She pushes her glasses up onto her nose. "But no luck?"

I'm about to tell her that I wasn't having problems and

didn't need the combination changed, when I remember what Britt said about Kathryn's mom being part of the school board. I figure it isn't worth it, and I'm still hoping to catch the bus so I don't have to get my dad involved.

"I guess not," I say, then go along with the lie. "But maybe I have the new combination wrong. Can you give it to me again?"

"Sure, hon." She pulls a binder off a shelf and leafs through it. I glance out into the hallway. Kids are still walking out, so the buses must not have left yet.

"Two fifty-six, two fifty-six," she says as she turns the pages.

I'm rocking back and forth on my feet, my heart rate increasing by ten beats every time she has to turn another page. I glance out at the hallway again. It's getting quieter.

"Ah! Here it is," she finally says, and scribbles the combination down on a Post-it.

"Thank you," I yell, as I sprint down the hallway toward my locker, weaving in and out of a few stragglers.

The hallway is empty when I get to my locker, and I quickly try the new combination. It works, and my locker springs open. I grab my jacket, throw my books in my backpack, slam the locker shut, and run for the exit.

I get there as soon as the last bus pulls away.

I can hear Kathryn and her Cronies giggling in my head. The tears that I refused to let loose all day finally escape and make their way down my cheeks.

"Hey." I hear a voice from behind me. I wipe my face with the back of my hand, and turn around to see Britt unlocking her bike from the bicycle rack.

"You okay?" She squints and lifts a hand to shield her eyes from the sun.

"Oh yeah, I'm fine," I say. "I—I just got lost coming out of school and missed my bus."

I can't tell her the truth. Then she'd want me to tell Mr. Russo that Kathryn's been messing with my locker too, and then maybe Mr. Russo would finally believe her. But if I do that, then the retribution would be worse than doing nothing. The way Kathryn treats me is bad, but it's nowhere near as bad as how she treats Britt.

"Do you need a ride home?" Britt asks, and then looks at her bike. "I mean, is there someone you can call?"

"I can call my dad," I say.

"Want me to wait for you?" She leans her bike up against the rack.

"No, thanks," I say, even though I do. "I'm sure you want to get out of here."

Britt stares at me for a second, then locks her bike back up. "Come on, let's go call your dad."

We get to the door of the main office, and Britt decides to wait in the hallway.

"You really don't want them to see you hanging out with me. It won't do anything good for your image."

I use the school phone to call my dad. I tell him the same story I told Britt—that I got lost and missed my bus. He tells me he's on his way.

Britt and I walk outside to wait.

"My dad could give you a ride," I tell her. "We could probably fit the bike in the car."

"No, thanks," Britt says. "I like riding home. Helps to clear my head."

I totally understand why she'd need stress relief after a day like this.

"You can go," I tell her. "My dad will be here any minute."

Britt unlocks her bike. "Okay, if you're sure."

I nod. "Positive. Anyway, we have tons of homework tonight. You might as well get started."

"Oh, joy," Britt says. "And that reminds me, we've got to work on that family tree thing."

"Yeah," I say. I'm kind of looking forward to working on it, now that I know Britt isn't as scary as she seems. "Maybe we can get together this weekend?"

"Maybe," Britt says, and she hops on her bike. "See you tomorrow."

About ten minutes later, Dad's car pulls into the school parking lot. He stops at the main entrance, and I open the door and climb into the passenger seat.

"Sorry to make you come out here." I put my backpack on the floor by my feet.

"That's okay. How was your day?" Dad's still wearing Grandad's overalls.

"It was fine." I smile. It's a totally fake smile, but luckily Dad doesn't notice.

"Are the kids nice?"

"Some are. Some aren't. You know. Same as everywhere else."

Dad nods. "I hear there's a PTA meeting tonight. I think I'm going to go."

"Why?" My voice comes out screechier than I mean it to.

"I've never had the chance to be involved in your schools. I thought it would be nice to learn more, now that I have some free time."

"I really don't think you're missing much, Dad." I stare out the window. I wonder if we pass Brody and Britt's house on our ride home. I don't see Britt on her bike, but maybe she made it home already.

"I want to," Dad says. "I think it will be good for all of us."

I purse my lips together. I can't imagine how Dad getting involved in my life will help me one single bit.

Dad comes home from the PTA meeting just as I'm finishing up my math homework. He looks different. Weird. I stare at him until I can figure it out.

He looks *happy*.

He sits next to me at the kitchen table. I finish the last of my worksheet, then put my books in my backpack for tomorrow.

"Want some tea before bed? Maybe a nice chamomile?" Dad gets up and fills the teakettle with water.

"Uhhhh, okay." I look at him closely to be sure he really is my dad and not some robot replacement.

Dad brings two steaming mugs over to the table. He sits down next to me and we sip our tea.

"You added honey and lemon?"

"I did. What do you think?"

"It's nice." I take another sip. "So how was the PTA meeting?"

"It was good." He takes a sip of tea and smiles. "Really good."

"What was so good about it?"

He purses his lips and sets his mug down. "Well, for one, it was nice to be able to learn more about your school and the curriculum. I hear you're learning Shakespeare?"

"Yeah, but we did that last semester at my old school."

"And there are all kinds of after-school clubs you might be interested in," Dad says.

"Maybe." I haven't even thought about after-school clubs. I have a feeling just making it through the regular day will be hard enough.

"And I got the chance to meet some of your classmates' parents."

"Mmmm-hmmm." I sip my tea. "That's nice."

"In fact, there's something I'd like to talk to you about." Dad plays with the tag on his tea bag.

"Yeah?" I wrap my hands around the warm mug.

"Well," Dad begins. He's staring into his tea. "I haven't really dated at all since your mom died."

Oh. Oh no. Oh no, no, no. Not this conversation. Is my Dad going to talk to me about his love life?

Now I stare into my teacup. I wonder if it's possible to dive in and swim away.

"I met someone tonight, and I'd like to ask her out to dinner."

I cringe and pull my mug in closer. "Ugh, Dad. Why are you telling me this?"

"Because I want to be sure it's okay with you."

"I don't want to know anything about your love life," I say, shaking my head. "Gross."

"It's not gross, Poppy. It's been a really long time since I've put myself out there."

I put my hands over my ears. "Oh please, Dad. I really don't want to hear about it."

"Don't worry." Dad smiles. "It's not like I'm going to give you any details."

"Ugggghhhhhh," I scream. "Please. Just stop."

"Okay, okay." Dad chuckles. "So I have your permission?"

"Yes, you have my permission to date anyone you want. As long as you don't tell me about it." I shudder.

Dad leans back in the chair and puts his arms behind his head. "It's a deal."

I give him a half smile.

"I'm really glad to hear you feel that way," he says. "I'm looking forward to getting to know her. I'm glad you're not weirded out because it's one of your classmates' mothers."

What?

I look up. "Whose mother is it?"

A huge grin spreads across his face. "Kathryn Woodruff's."

CHAPTER 8

DON'T REACT. DON'T REACT. DON'T REACT.

I say the words over and over again in my head. If I react, Dad will wonder why. And I can't tell him why because this Dad, this New Dad, is trying way too hard to be part of my life. If he knew the truth—that Kathryn was the devil in a dress—he'd want to talk about it. And talk to the principal. And maybe even—yikes—talk to her mother.

I purse my lips together and keep my face looking as normal as possible. I take a sip of tea.

"Do you know her?" Dad asks.

I nod. "Yeah. She showed me around today."

"That's terrific. Her mom tells me she's quite the student."

I shrug. "I don't know her that well."

"Hopefully, she's as wonderful as her mother says she is."

Don't react.

"Hopefully."

"Well, kiddo." Dad stands up. "I'm going to get ready for bed. Farmers get up early, you know!"

"Uhhhhh, sure, Dad." I hope my dad knows that dressing in overalls does not make him a farmer. "I'll be up soon."

"Good night, Poppy." Dad kisses the top of my head. Which is weird, since he hasn't kissed me good night since I was seven. But this is New Dad. New Dad kisses his daughter good night.

After I wash my tea mug, I get ready for bed myself. I bring my phone, and text Amanda under the covers.

Mandy: How was the 1st day?

Me: :(

Mandy: ????

Me: The kids.

Mandy: Oh no! Hillbillies?!

Me: Worse. Mean girls.

Mandy: Ouch.

Me: Yep.

Mandy: Cute boys?

Me: One.

Mandy: Come home.

Me: Not yet. Luv u.

Mandy: Luv u too. Good luck tmro.

Me: Gnite

I set my alarm, but I can't sleep. I feel like the metal box in my underwear drawer is burning a hole in my dresser. Would it be so bad to ignore Mom's request, just this once?

Yes. Yes, it would be so bad. My mother hasn't asked anything from me in five years.

Get a grip, Poppy.

I flip over so I'm facing the wall. I hope this week goes by fast.

I spend the next few days ignoring everyone. I stay far away from Kathryn, I eat lunch in the library, and I'm sure to be the first one on the bus so I can sit right behind the bus driver. Although my life is pretty boring, my plan seems to be working.

On Thursday, I get dressed and debate whether or not to put my hair in a ponytail. I decide against it, because I don't want to look like I'm trying to look like everyone else. Instead, I pull my hair into a headband—a pink one that matches the tips of my hair—and add a pair of feather earrings. I throw on some blue jeans and a pink sweater, and take one last glance in the mirror. I think I look perfectly normal, but I'm sure Kathryn will find something wrong with me.

Dad's already in the kitchen by the time I get there. He's standing at the stove, doing something—cooking? And what's he wearing? I get closer and see that it's an apron, and it says, REAL MEN COOK.

"Good morning." Dad is way too perky. "I made us some oatmeal."

I stare blankly at him.

"Want some?" He gestures to the bubbling pot of oats in front of him.

I blink.

"Poppy?" Dad raises his eyebrows. "You okay?"

I nod. "I didn't know you knew how to cook."

"Well." Dad laughs. "It's oatmeal. I'm not sure if that counts as cooking, but yeah, I've been known to whip some things together for a tasty meal."

"Hmmm," I say, because I don't know what else to say. I think maybe Dad's possessed. This house is haunted, after all. I squint my eyes at him, trying to see if there's someone else's aura surrounding him, but he just looks like Dad.

Troy comes running down the stairs and into the kitchen.

"What smells so good?" Troy likes food almost as much as he likes his truck.

"Oatmeal. Want some?" Dad stirs the pot.

"Yeah!" Troy grabs a bowl from the cabinet and hands it to Dad, not the least bit concerned that Dad has never, not once, made breakfast.

Then again, Troy wouldn't notice if his own eyebrows were on fire.

"What are you staring at?" Troy looks at me and sticks out his tongue.

I roll my eyes and try to force down the oatmeal, which is both undercooked and burnt at the same time. I scrape out the remnants of my bowl when dad isn't looking. I throw a granola bar into my backpack and trek down the driveway to the bus stop. Another day. I can do this. I'm sure Mom has a plan for me.

As it's done every day this week, my heart does a little flutter when the bus climbs up the hill. As it stops in front of me, I start my new daily ritual. I take a deep breath, lift my head a little higher, and step on. I slide right into the seat just behind the bus driver, which, thankfully, has been empty since the second day of school.

Bonus: Since I'm so close to the door, I'm the first one off the bus when it pulls into school. I've already memorized my new locker combination, and I head straight there. I just have to stay out of everybody's way until . . . well, until I move out of this town (not likely to happen anytime soon with New Dad making the decisions).

Maybe New Dad will let me homeschool.

For the third day in a row, I'm the first one to homeroom. Mrs. Simmons smiles at me when I walk in.

"Good morning, Poppy. Finding your way around okay?"

"Yes, thank you." I take my seat and pull out my schedule. Mrs. Simmons nods and goes back to sipping something out of her to-go cup.

First period this morning is Intro to Agriculture. Maybe I'll learn something about Mom and her roses.

Kathryn and Emily glide into homeroom. I sink down in my chair. Kathryn glances at Mrs. Simmons, and then stops at my desk. This is a first. For the past few days, she's just smiled (first checking to see that Mrs. Simmons was looking, of course) and continued on to her seat.

"Goodness, Poppy!" She puts her hand on my arm. "I missed you all week. Why haven't you been waiting for me?"

I look past Kathryn at Mrs. Simmons, who's looking at us behind her to-go mug.

"Oh, I guess you've been such a good host that I already know my way around." I give her a smile so big, she can probably see my tonsils.

She just stares at me, and I wonder if her mom told her about meeting my dad. I shudder just thinking about it. The thought of Dad dating is gross enough. But the thought of him dating Kathryn's mom? Chock-full of gross.

Brody walks in and stops at my desk, directly behind Kathryn.

"What's the matter, I smell or something?" He smiles at me. "You didn't sit with me on the bus again."

My ears get hot. "Oh, sorry. Guess I didn't see you."

"That's what you said yesterday," Brody points out.

"I was just telling Poppy that she should have waited for us," Kathryn tells Brody.

"Yeah." Brody nods. "Don't forget about us next time."

"Okay," I say. But as soon as the bell rings, I bolt out of homeroom and sprint to class. I'm the first one there.

"Welcome," the teacher says. "I'm Mrs. Quinn. You must be Poppy."

"Yes, nice to meet you," I tell her. Mrs. Quinn looks like she could be anywhere from fifty to eighty. She wears her glasses on a chain around her neck, and her gray hair is pinned neatly in a bun. She has a warm smile, and I instantly like her.

Mrs. Quinn tells me I can sit anywhere, so I find an empty seat at the back of the classroom. Intro to

Agriculture is something I didn't even know existed until this week, and even though I get a good vibe from Mrs. Quinn, I figure the farther away I am from the teacher for this class, the better.

I pull my notebook open and stare at the blank page. I write *Intro to Agriculture* at the top, and I doodle some roses in the corners.

I don't notice Brody until he stops at my desk.

"Cool, you're in this class," he says.

I glance around but don't see Kathryn. Maybe I'll get lucky and actually have one class without her. "Yep, I thought it would be fun."

Brody sits down in the desk next to mine. "It's the best class ever."

"Really?" I ask. "What kind of stuff do you do? Do you, like, learn about flowers?"

Brody shrugs. "Sure, sometimes. But it depends on what your project is for the 4-H fair."

I blink. He just stares at me, so I nod like I know what he's talking about.

"You don't know what a 4-H fair is, do you?"

My face feels like it's going to explode. I come clean because I wouldn't even know how to fake this. The first time I ever heard of it was in Mom's letter. "Not entirely."

Brody laughs. "That's okay, you're a city girl."

I smile. He says it in a nice way.

"4-H is kind of a youth group run by the USDA." When I don't respond, he adds, "The United States Department of Agriculture."

"Ahhhh." I nod. Even though I'm not entirely sure what that is either.

"The 4-H fair is in June, and everybody in this class is assigned to do a project that's presented at the fair."

"That's cool." I glance past him at the kids streaming in. Still no sign of Kathryn.

"Yeah, I'm doing my project on Peter."

I try to remember meeting a Peter. "I don't think I know him."

Brody pushes his hair out of his eyes and laughs. "Peter Cottontail. My rabbit."

I raise my eyebrows. "You have a rabbit named Peter Cottontail?"

"Not very original, I know." Now Brody's face looks red. I stare down at my desk.

"So what are you going to do with Peter? Pull him out of a hat?"

"Hmmm. Not a bad idea." Brody laughs. "But no. I'm building him a house."

"That's awesome. I have no idea what I should do my project on." I don't have any rabbits.

"There are a ton of options," Brody says. "Thomas does one on dairy production, Cheryl's is on wind power, and Kathryn's growing roses."

My head snaps up. "Roses?"

"Yeah, she does the same project every year." He rolls his eyes. "And she wins the blue ribbon every year."

"Can I do that? Can I grow roses?"

Brody squints at me. "Sure, I guess so. Do you grow roses?"

"Not yet." I lean forward in my chair. "But I'm going to start."

And at that very instant I know. I know why Mom sent me here.

CHAPTER 9

"I HATE TO BREAK IT TO YOU," BRODY SAYS. "BUT there's no way you could start growing roses now and have them ready for the fair."

My mouth goes dry as dirt. "I can't?"

"No, they take way more time than that to grow."

"They do?"

"Yeah. Kathryn's been growing roses forever."

"Did I hear my name?" Kathryn and Emily are right in front of me. I guess I was too interested in the possibility of following in my mother's footsteps to see them come in.

Brody looks up at her. "I was just telling Poppy about your roses."

Kathryn crinkles her nose. "Why?"

"Because she was thinking about growing roses for the fair."

Kathryn looks at me like I just smacked her in the face with her own ponytail. "*You* grow roses?"

"Well, no," I sputter. "I just . . . I thought it would be cool to learn how."

Kathryn just smirks. "Good luck with that."

She takes a seat on the other side of Brody, and Emily dutifully sits down next to her.

I think about what Brody said, and wonder exactly how long roses do take to grow. I'm positive this is what I'm supposed to be doing. I'm sure Mom sent me here to grow roses, to help her with her flowers that she had so much trouble with.

"Okay, class." Mrs. Quinn stands up in front of the room. "Today you're going to work on your 4-H project outline. You can use the computers in the back of the room for reference. But *only* for reference."

Most of the kids get up and head for the computers. Some open books, and some whisper to each other.

Just as I'm wondering what to do with myself, Mrs. Quinn calls me over to her desk.

"So, Poppy," she begins. "Each student is preparing a project for the 4-H fair in June."

I nod, since now I know what a 4-H fair is.

"Is there something you might be interested in working on?"

"Well," I say. "I'd like to learn more about roses."

"Fabulous!" Mrs. Quinn clasps her hands together. "I could partner you up with Kathryn—"

"Oh no. I, uhhhh," I stammer. "I wouldn't want to intrude on her project. Is there something I can do myself?"

Mrs. Quinn purses her lips together. "Well, you can certainly grow roses, but they wouldn't be ready in time for the fair. Is there anything else that interests you?"

"I don't know much about agriculture," I say. "I moved here from the city."

"That's okay!" Mrs. Quinn smiles. "There are plenty of agricultural activities in cities, too. There are parks, potted plants, windowsill herbs. Lots of exciting projects!"

Mrs. Quinn is obviously very enthusiastic about agriculture. I wish I felt the same way about something other than roses.

"Can I think about it?" I ask. I need more time to figure out what Mom wants me to do, given that roses will take more time than I have.

"Sure," Mrs. Quinn says. "Why don't you let me know after spring break? Meantime, feel free to use one of the computers to research ideas."

I find an empty computer and Google "roses." There are two hundred and fifty million entries. I sigh.

"You might as well forget about it," a voice behind me says.

I turn around to find Kathryn standing over me.

"It takes years of practice to grow roses, and clearly you don't have the first idea where to begin."

"Well, I've got to start somewhere." I turn back to the computer.

"Don't waste your time." Kathryn lowers her voice and bends down to whisper in my ear. "You don't belong here, Poppy. So don't try to act like you do."

Before I can turn around and say something back, she struts away.

I remind myself, for the hundredth time today, that I don't care about Kathryn. I'm not here to make friends. I'm here because my mom wants me to be here. For some reason that I can't yet figure out.

Maybe I can plant roses now and be in next year's fair. Maybe that's Mom's plan. I don't have to win this year's fair, do I?

Regardless, I have to find something to do for this year's project. I Google "4-H fair" for some ideas. Let's see . . . rabbit show, goat demonstration, woodworking, beekeeping . . .

I suddenly realize how useless my city talents—navigating the subway, weaving in and out of crowded streets, finding the Starbucks with the shortest line—are here. I'm pretty sure I'm going to fail Intro to Agriculture. I just hope I don't fail Mom, too.

The bell rings, and I'm still no closer to finding a project. I quickly gather my books and shoot out the door before Kathryn or Brody can see me. I pretty much make this my goal for the day (and my life), and by the end of the morning I've barely spoken to them. I feel a weird combination of sadness and relief every time I manage to avoid Brody. I really want to talk to him, but I'm not sure it's worth the risk. I have a feeling I've seen only a portion of Kathryn's wicked ways. I'm not sure I can handle the full load.

I've been going to the library instead of going to lunch, but today I'm really hungry. Since Kathryn's been leaving me alone for the last few days, I decide to go to the cafeteria. I sit at the same table I sat at on my first day, but Britt isn't there. I get the pizza and eat it by myself.

As soon as I take the last bite of pizza, I see Brody walking my way. I check my teeth with my tongue to be sure I don't have cheese sticking out of them.

"Why are you sitting alone?" He pulls out the chair next to mine and sits down.

"Oh." I look around the room. "This is just where I sit, I guess."

"Where's Britt?"

"I don't know," I say. "I haven't seen her all day."

Brody purses his lips. "She probably stayed home."

I shrug. Britt is nice to me, and I'm thankful that someone is. But I can't worry about her or anyone else. I have too many other things to think about.

"Well, you could sit with me if you want." He looks at me then quickly looks away. "I mean, with Kathryn and the rest of us."

I try to laugh, but it comes out more like a snort. "Thanks, but I think I'm safer here."

Brody looks at me like he's not sure what I'm talking about. Is it possible that he doesn't even realize how mean Kathryn is?

"Well, the invitation is open." Brody stands up. "In case you change your mind."

I glance past him and sure enough, Kathryn is glaring at me. Great. I'm back on her radar. She looks like she's ready to pounce at any minute, just waiting to stab me in the eyes with the tip of her ponytail.

"Thanks." I give him a slight smile, and he goes back to his table of popular kids.

I spend the remainder of the lunch period tearing

apart my napkin. When the bell finally rings, I scoop up my book, throw my garbage away, and sprint to my next class. I have to stay ahead of Kathryn at all times. If I'm in the classroom and within earshot of teachers, she at least has to be nice to me.

My plan works. I stay away from her all day, and she's on the bus before I get there. Lucky for me, the seat behind the bus driver is empty again. I crouch down in the bench, take a deep breath, and close my eyes.

Which is why I don't notice that the bus driver missed my spot until we're well past my house.

"Excuse me." I lean forward in my seat so the bus driver can hear me. "I think we passed my house."

"Yes, but I thought you were going home with a friend?" The bus driver glances at me in his mirror.

"I—what?" I have no idea what he's talking about.

"Kathryn back there told me you were going home with Cindy. Hers is the last stop," the bus driver says.

I turn around to find Kathryn and Emily laughing like hyenas at the back of the bus.

I can feel my blood heating up, and if blood could actually boil, I'm pretty sure mine would be boiling over.

"Oh yes, I forgot," I tell the bus driver. Two can play her game. "But she had it wrong. I'm not going home with Cindy. I'm going to Brody Fuller's house."

"Okay, then," the bus driver says. "His stop is next."

I smile. Because I can't wait to see Kathryn's face when I walk off the bus with Brody.

CHAPTER 10

THE BUS STOPS, AND I GLANCE BACK TO SEE BRODY standing up. Kathryn and Emily are giggling at each other and waving at him.

"See you tomorrow," Brody says as he passes by my seat.

That's what he thinks.

I grab my backpack and follow him off the bus. I turn around just in time to see Kathryn's nostrils flare to three times their normal size.

"What?" Brody looks around as the bus drives away. "What are you doing here?"

Now that I'm here, I'm not sure myself. What was I thinking? That was really stupid of me. Not only do I have no way home, but Kathryn's going to make my life absolutely miserable after this.

"Poppy?" Brody waves his hand in front of my face.

I sigh. "The bus driver missed my stop."

"That stinks," Brody says. "Why didn't you just ask him to go back?"

I don't want to tell him what happened. Then he'll go back to Kathryn and that will make things even worse than they already are.

"By the time I realized it, we were at your stop. And since it's the next closest one to mine, I figured I'd just get off here."

Brody smiles. "That's cool."

"It is?" I raise an eyebrow.

"Well, yeah." He looks down at his foot, which is kicking at a lump of dirt. "You never seem to want to talk to me at school."

I feel like I just swallowed the lump of dirt. I don't want Brody to think I don't like him. But with Kathryn always lurking, I just can't take the chance. Of course, none of that matters now. I'm sure Kathryn's plotting her revenge right this very minute.

I'm trying to figure out how to tell Brody that it's not that I don't want to talk to him at school, when Britt comes zooming by on her bike.

"Hey," she says to me. "What are you doing here?"

Brody spins to face her. "Where were you today?"

Britt shrugs. "Home."

"Does Mom know you missed school?" Brody's smile is gone.

"Yeah." Britt is glaring at Brody. "I told her before she left for work that I wasn't feeling good."

"You look fine to me," Brody says.

"Well, I'm feeling better."

"Did you even get your homework?" Brody asks.

"That's not your problem," Britt spits. I feel like I'm spying on a conversation I shouldn't be hearing.

"If Mom gets stressed, then it's my problem."

"Mom isn't going to get stressed. I'm doing fine in school."

"You skipped today! How is that doing fine?"

"I was sick!"

"Whatever," Brody says, then turns to me. "Sorry."

"No, it's okay. I have a brother." I look at both of them and give a small smile. "I totally get it."

"So, do you guys have a date or something?" Britt asks. She doesn't say it in a mean way at all, but Brody must think she does, because his ears turn bright red.

"I just missed my stop," I say before he can answer her.

"You're not having much bus luck, huh?" Britt smiles.

"I'm still trying to figure the whole thing out."

"Are you hungry? We have snacks." Britt turns her

bike around so she's heading back down the gravel driveway. "Come on."

"Sorry about her," Brody mumbles as we walk toward the house.

"You don't have to be sorry," I say. "I like your sister."

Brody's eyes shoot up. I can't tell if he's pleasantly surprised or just surprised. He opens the gate of the white picket fence, and leads me to the front porch. There's a swing hanging next to the front door, overlooking the lawn. I follow Brody into the house, and we meet Britt in the kitchen. Their house is small, but every room looks like it came from a "Beautiful Homes" board on Pinterest. There are flower arrangements on the dining room table, colorful beeswax candlesticks in the living room, and what looks like a very expensive wooden coatrack in the foyer.

"This is a great house," I say. "Such amazing decorations."

"Yeah." Britt looks around. "Our mom loves to do crafts and stuff. She made most of the things in the house."

"She made this stuff?" I point to the coatrack. "Even that?"

Britt laughs. "That one took her a few months."

"It's amazing," I say. "Is that what she does for work?"

Britt's expression changes. Her smile fades, and her eyes dim a little. "No, she works at the factory now."

"Now?" I ask.

"Well, she used to sell her stuff, but when my dad left she had to get a more steady job." "Oh." I look down at my feet. "I'm sorry. I mean, that your dad left."

Britt shrugs. "It's okay. It was a long time ago. He—"

"Jeez, Britt," Brody interrupts her. "I'm sure Poppy doesn't want to hear about our lame family life."

"Oh no, it's okay," I say. "I could even—"

"Want a cookie?" Brody shoves a plate of chocolate chips in my face.

"Yeah, sure." I take a cookie. "Thanks."

"Be careful," Britt whispers as Brody goes to the refrigerator for some milk. "He only likes to talk about happy things."

"It's pretty nice outside," Brody says. "Let's go sit there."

We go out the back door and onto a patio. I hold my breath when I look beyond it.

It's the most incredible garden I've ever seen.

There are rows and rows of flowers—tulips and daffodils and lilacs and *roses*—and they're all amazing.

"Is this your mom's garden?" I walk to the edge of the patio and stare out at the garden.

"No." Britt comes to stand next to me. "It's ours." She points to Brody, then back to herself.

I turn to look at her so fast I think my head might fall

off. "Yours?" Britt does not look like the kind of person who gardens.

"And yours?" I look at Brody. He's pulling blades of grass out of the ground.

"Yeah, it's kind of a hobby, but don't tell anyone at school," Brody says.

"Okaaaaay," I say. "But why?"

Britt rolls her eyes. "He doesn't think gardening is cool enough for him."

"That's not it." Brody puts a blade of grass between his fingers and whistles. "It's just that . . . my friends wouldn't understand."

I walk out to the roses. I probably should ask permission, but I can't help myself. It's like they're pulling me over to them and I have no will of my own.

"Who planted these?"

"Those are mine." Britt nods. "Brody doesn't have the patience for roses."

"Are you going to enter these into the 4-H fair?" I ask.

"Ummmmm, no." Britt bites her lower lip. "I don't do the 4-H fair."

"Why not?" My hands fly into the air. "You'd totally win."

"Competition's really not my thing," Britt says. "And besides, the judges are so . . . judgy."

Before I can say another word, Brody interrupts us. He's holding out a phone.

"Hey, shouldn't you call your parents or something? Tell them you're here?"

Oh no! I forgot about that. I don't know how New Dad is going to react to me coming home late. Old Dad never would have noticed.

I take the phone and dial Dad's cell. He answers on the first ring. I tell him I went home with a friend, and he tells me to call him when I'm ready for a ride, but to make sure it's before dinner because he's trying out a new recipe.

New Dad is so weird.

I hand the phone back to Brody, and then turn to Britt. "Can you teach me how to plant roses?"

"Why do you want to plant roses?" Brody asks. "You can't grow them in time for the fair."

"I know," I say. "I just—I really want to learn how."

I can't tell them why I want to know. I can't tell them that my dead mother is sending me a message from beyond the grave, and I'm pretty sure she wants me to avenge her roses. I can't tell them that because it sounds crazy.

Even though I'm pretty sure it's true.

"Don't you have a garden at home?" Britt asks.

"We did. Once," I say. "But there's nothing there now. I'd love to start one."

"Maybe we can help." Brody looks at Britt.

"You guys would do that?" I'm sure this was a ton of work and took a lot of time. Why would they want to have to do it again, for someone they hardly know?

"Sure," Britt says. "But you're going to have to be willing to keep it up."

"Oh, I will," I say. "Maybe you can come over sometime?"

Britt and Brody look at each other and nod.

YES! I'm going to grow roses.

CHAPTER 11

MY ALARM GOES OFF EARLY ON FRIDAY MORNING.

Finally Friday!

Letter day!

I throw the covers off me and stumble for my dresser. I pull open my underwear drawer, take out the metal box, and bring it back with me to bed.

I crawl back under the covers and yank out the letter marked #3.

A photo flutters out, and I quickly grab it off my bedspread. It's a picture of a rosebush—a dry, wilting, sad-looking rosebush.

Poor Mom.

I lean back on my pillow and begin reading the letter.

April 27, 1985

Dear Poppy,

School was the worst today. THE WORST. Tammy Griffin hates me, and I'm pretty sure it's because I had the nerve to talk to Brian.

I made it to the library last weekend, and guess who I ran into? Did you guess Brian? Yes? Ding, ding, ding, ding! You're the million-dollar winner!

He was there looking at books for our social studies report. When he saw me come in, he actually walked over to me and asked if I could help him find a book on Abraham Lincoln! Of course, I tried to play it cool, but you know I was totally wigging out! I found him a book, and he thanked me. Then I didn't know what else to say, so I walked away. WHY AM I SUCH A DORK AROUND CUTE BOYS?!

So when I saw Brian in the hall today I was determined to actually talk to him. I asked him how he liked the book on Abe Lincoln (lame question, I know). Tammy must have heard me, because she told everybody that I was a total nerd who spends her weekends at the library reading about old dead guys. I pretended like it didn't bother me, but of course it did. I don't want Brian to think I'm a complete geek.

To make things worse, I can't figure out how to save my roses. I'm not sure they'll have enough time for them to recover (I included a pic so you could see how bad they look). They have to recover, Poppy. They just have to. I have to beat Tammy at the 4-H fair. I wish you were here. Together, we'd definitely win that blue ribbon and put Tammy in her place. I can dream, right?!

Off to watch GROWING PAINS. Kirk Cameron looks soooooooo much like Brian!

Until next week.

Love & friendship always & forever,
Daphne

I type "Kirk Cameron" into the Google bar of my phone. He was the star of *Growing Pains*, which was a TV show when Mom was my age. He was kinda cute. I guess. And bonus: Now I know what Brian looked like.

I laugh. I can't believe Mom—my beautiful, confident, lovable mother—was ever shy around boys. The crazy thing is . . . I'm shy around boys too! Who knew we had this in common? Plus, Mom had trouble with mean girls too. Maybe that's why she wrote these letters. So I could see that I'm not alone.

I quickly grab the notebook I keep on my nightstand and scribble a note back.

Dear Mom,

I had a terrible day too! There's this girl, Kathryn, who sounds just as mean as Tammy. She's known me for less than two weeks, but decided to hate me anyway. She told me I don't belong here, and that I'm not allowed to talk to Brody (a really cute boy who's nice AND friendly).

And it's not like Brody's my boyfriend or anything. Not that I've ever had a boyfriend. The only thing I know about boys I learned from Troy, which means all I know about boys is that they eat a lot, play Minecraft (that's a video game), tell fart jokes, and torture their younger sisters. But Brody seems—I don't know—different. Maybe more like Brian. He and his sister, Britt, have an awesome garden and they said they'd help me with mine! So there's still hope for my roses!

Anyway, it totally sounds to me like Brian liked you! Not that it matters, because as you know, you grew up to marry Dad. I wonder if you ever wondered what happened to Brian. So Tammy's just being a jerk to you for no reason. Just like Kathryn's being a jerk to me for no reason.

You want to hear the worst part? I'm not even sure I should tell you this (although you probably know because spirits know everything), but Dad wants to ask Kathryn's mom out to dinner! Before you feel bad about that, you should know that he hasn't dated anybody since you died. He was really sad and just worked all the time so he wouldn't have to think about it.

Love ya,
Poppy

PS: I hope Kathryn's mom is a lot nicer than she is.

I throw on some jeans and a T-shirt, and shove a cardigan in my backpack in case it gets cold. I purposely move as slowly as possible. Maybe if I miss the bus, Dad will drive me to school. After going home with Brody yesterday, I especially need to keep my distance from Kathryn today.

Some incredible smell is wafting up the stairs, and I follow it to find Dad in the kitchen, once again wearing his REAL MEN COOK apron on top of his overalls. And he's humming.

"Good morning," he says when he sees me. "Bacon and eggs?"

I glance in the frying pan, and even though I'm skeptical after the oatmeal Dad made, my mouth waters. "You've graduated from oatmeal?"

Dad laughs. "You probably don't remember, but I used to cook all the time before . . ."

His voice trails off, but I know what he was going to say. Before Mom died. Maybe she got him that apron?

"Well, it smells good." I grab a plate out of the cupboard. "Better load me up before Troy gets down here."

"I heard that," Troy says, barreling down the steps. "You better save some for me!"

Troy pats Dad on the back, and they do some kind of man-handshake thing that I've never seen before. Then they laugh and laugh.

Where am I?

This is not my life. Or at least, it wasn't before. My life before was waking up, getting dressed, meeting Mandy in front of Starbucks on Tenth Street at 7:10, picking up a muffin and a mocha latte, which I ate and drank on my walk to school. I bought lunch at the cafeteria, Mandy and I walked home together, did our homework at either her apartment or mine, and then I grabbed a slice of pizza or Chinese takeout for dinner. I didn't see Dad. I hardly saw Troy.

And now we're all sitting down eating breakfast together? And Dad's cooking?

I take a bite of scrambled eggs. *Wow. Oh, wow.* These are actually good. A lot better than the oatmeal disaster. Soft but not mushy, and seasoned with just the right amount of salt and pepper. I close my eyes, and for a second, I swear I could smell mint tea.

My eyes shoot open and I look around, fully expecting to see Mom—or at least the ghost of Mom—standing over me. It would make perfect sense! Who else could orchestrate a breakfast like this? Who else could turn Old Dad into New Dad?

But there's no sign of her.

Instead, Dad's standing next to me with a teapot.

"Want some tea?" he asks. "It's mint, your favorite."

I look at him, searching for some kind of realization that mint tea was Mom's favorite too. But he looks pretty normal. I mean, except for the crazy apron.

"Ummmm, sure, Dad." He pours me a cup, and I figure tea drinking is a nice, slow activity. One that will surely cause me to miss the bus.

In an effort to distract Dad from the time, I try to have a real conversation with him—something I can't remember doing since, well, since ever.

"So, Dad," I say in between bites of bacon, "my friends are going to help me plant a garden here. Is that okay?"

Dad puts his tea mug down on the table. "I didn't know you were into gardening, Poppy."

I shrug. "It's something I'd like to try."

Dad looks really closely at me, his blue eyes all sparkly. "I think that's a great idea."

His mouth opens like he's about to say more, but he just gets this spacey look on his face, like he's thinking about something that's very far away.

"I know you've been wanting to do some farming." I blow on my tea. "So I wanted to ask you where I can have my garden."

Dad looks out the window. "What about in the back, next to the barn? I seem to remember a long time ago, Grandad had a huge garden there."

"Hey, Dad," Troy says, with his mouth full. "Can I build a racetrack for my truck?"

"Let's work on getting your driver's license first, okay, buddy?" Dad gives Troy a light punch on the shoulder.

I glance at the clock. Two minutes until the bus comes. If I want to miss it, I have to keep the conversation alive, so I blurt out the first thing I think of.

"Did you know Mom grew roses?"

Dad stops drinking his tea midsip, and Troy drops his fork.

Nobody has spoken Mom's name out loud in years.

The room is so quiet, that I'm pretty sure I could hear the rumble of the bus up the hill. If Dad or Troy notice, they don't say anything. I think they're stunned into silence.

"I mean, I kind of remember her telling me that," I say.

"Wow, Poppy." Dad smiles. "I can't believe you remember something like that. It was so long ago."

Oh no. What if I blew it? What if he knows there's no way I'd remember something from that long ago? What if he finds the letters and—

"But you must have a pretty good memory, because you're right." Dad holds his tea mug tightly and inhales.

"I kind of remember that too," Troy says. "She had a ton of flowers out on our balcony in the city."

Dad nods. "She did. In fact, we couldn't fit furniture out there because there were so many."

Troy laughs. "Yeah, I remember that."

I stare down at my tea. I wish I remembered that. Troy was ten when she died, so he probably remembers a lot more than I do. But we don't talk about her. We've never talked about her.

A huge lump is growing in my throat. I take a big gulp of tea to try to push it down.

"Oh, hey." Dad looks like he snapped out of whatever had him possessed. "Look at the time."

I glance at the clock on the stove. "Uh-oh," I say, trying my best to sound disappointed. "I think I missed the bus."

"It's okay. I'll give you a ride." Dad gets up and grabs his keys off the key hook hanging near the door. "You ready?"

"Yep." I pick up my backpack and head out to the car.

I sit in the front seat, and neither of us says anything for most of the ride. I wonder if Dad's thinking about Mom, like I am. I wonder if being in the house brings back memories for him, too. I want to ask him, but I don't. I'm still not sure exactly how to act around New Dad. But for the first time in a long time, I'm looking forward to figuring it out.

Dad drops me off, and I weave in and out of the kids coming off the buses. I just need to go to my locker and get to class without Kathryn seeing me. Thank goodness it's the Friday before spring break, and I'll have a whole nine days off before I have to do this again.

I shuffle along the hallway, keeping my head down the entire way. A weird smell wafts through the air, and the closer I get, the worse it is. The stink makes my eyes tear, and when I reach my locker, my stomach lurches.

My locker door is open.

And it's filled, top to bottom, with cow manure.

CHAPTER 12

HALF OF THE MIDDLE SCHOOL IS HUDDLED AROUND MY locker. The boys are cracking up, and the girls look like they're going to hurl.

"Whose locker is that, anyway?" somebody asks.

And at that minute, Kathryn comes running up to me. "Oh my goodness, Poppy!" She puts her arm around my shoulder. "Isn't that your locker?"

I squeeze my eyes shut and take a deep breath. I have to keep it together. I can't let her know she got to me.

I nod.

"Why would somebody do that to your locker?" Kathryn purses her lips as if she's actually pondering the question.

"I have no idea," I whisper.

"Does anyone know who pooped Poppy's locker?" She says it so everybody in the entire school can hear. I know she did it on purpose. So everyone would know that it's my locker.

A group of boys laugh. "Poopy Poppy," they say.

Great. Now I will forever be known as Poopy Poppy.

"What the—" Brody squeezes into the crowd. "What happened?"

"That's what we're trying to figure out." Kathryn makes a pouty face. "Who could have done this to Poppy's locker?"

"Holy—" Brody begins, but he's interrupted by Mr. Russo.

"Okay, everybody, back to class." He waves his arms and scurries the onlookers away. "Go, go, go. The bell is going to ring any minute now, and I won't be issuing late passes."

Kids scurry away, excitedly whispering to each other all the way to homeroom.

"Poppy, why don't you come with me." Mr. Russo gives me a halfhearted smile, and I follow him down the hallway.

"Mr. Russo," Kathryn calls after him. "Is there anything I can do to help?"

Mr. Russo stops and turns around. "I don't know, Kathryn. Did you see anything?"

"Well." Kathryn tilts her head, and her ponytail falls to one side. "I think I might have."

"Then by all means, come with us to my office."

Kathryn and I follow Mr. Russo into his office, and he closes the door behind him. He motions for us to sit down.

"Poppy, do you have any idea why anyone might have done this to your locker?"

I glance at Kathryn, who's looking at me with eyes the size of volleyballs. I quickly calculate the consequences of telling Mr. Russo that the only person who might have done this to my locker is Kathryn.

1) He won't believe me. Kathryn goes out of her way to act sweet and caring in front of all teachers. 2) Her mom is on the school board, which makes her Mr. Russo's boss. 3) My dad. He seems so happy, and I know he wants to ask Kathryn's mom out to dinner. And who knows, maybe Kathryn's mom is actually a nice person? Maybe her jerkiness isn't genetic. Doesn't my dad at least deserve a glimmer of hope at a love life, even if the thought of it makes me feel a little queasy?

Both Mr. Russo and Kathryn are staring at me, waiting for an answer.

"I can't think of anybody," I mumble.

Out of the corner of my eye, I see a smirk come over Kathryn's face. I quickly look down at my shoes.

"And what did you see, Kathryn?" Mr. Russo asks.

"Well, I can't tell for sure, but I could have sworn I saw someone hanging around Poppy's locker at dismissal yesterday. It looked like they were, you know, scoping it out."

"And do you know who that person was?" Mr. Russo raises an eyebrow at Kathryn.

Kathryn squirms in her chair and folds her hands in her lap. "I'd rather not say, Mr. Russo. I really don't want to get anyone in trouble."

Mr. Russo gives Kathryn a compassionate nod. "I understand. Nobody wants to tell on their classmates. But this is very important."

"I know," Kathryn says, looking up at Mr. Russo. "I want to do the right thing. . . ."

"The right thing is to let me know who you saw." Mr. Russo takes off his glasses. "The person who did this may be troubled, and if we find out who it is, we can help."

"Well, as long as I know it's going to help someone . . ." Kathryn bites her lip. I look at Mr. Russo, and he's nodding. I can't believe he's falling for this act.

Kathryn sighs. Loudly. "It was Britt Fuller. She was lurking by Poppy's locker yesterday."

"What?" I stand up. "That's impossible. Britt wasn't even in school yesterday."

"I know," Kathryn says. "That's why I even noticed it. It seemed really weird."

"Thank you for telling me, Kathryn," Mr. Russo says. "You did the right thing."

"But it wasn't her!" I say. "I'm sure of it."

"I'm not saying she did it," Kathryn says. "I'm only saying I saw her by your locker."

"I know for a fact she was home yesterday. She wasn't feeling well." I look at Mr. Russo.

"We'll talk to her," he says.

"It wasn't her," I say again. "She wouldn't do that."

"I'm glad you are supporting Ms. Fuller," Mr. Russo says. "But I think it's fair to say that you only just met her. You really don't know what she would or wouldn't do. We need to investigate all the leads we can."

Hot tears sting my eyes. I can't let Britt get in trouble for this. I know it was Kathryn. I absolutely know it.

But I can't prove it.

"I'm sure this is upsetting, Poppy." Mr. Russo hands me a tissue, and I realize tears are streaming down my face. "This is not what you want during your first week at a new school. We'll get to the bottom of it."

I dab the corners of my eyes with the tissue. I refuse to look at Kathryn. She's probably getting way too much pleasure out of this.

"Kathryn, why don't you head to class?" Mr. Russo says. "Poppy, you can stay here for a few more minutes."

Panic crosses Kathryn's face. "Are you sure you don't want me to stay and wait with her?"

"No, go on. She may need some more time, and there's no reason for you to miss any more class."

I get a glimmer of satisfaction at knowing that Kathryn's worried that I might tell Mr. Russo that I think it's her. And if I had some proof, even a sliver of evidence, I would.

"Is there anything you want to tell me, Poppy?" Mr. Russo sits in the chair Kathryn was just in. "Privately?"

I look up at him for a split second. He looks kind, like he might even understand . . .

But what if he doesn't? That's not a risk I can take.

"No," I finally say. "There's nothing."

"Okay." He leans back in his chair. "Stay here for as long as you'd like. I'll write you a late pass whenever you're ready to go to class."

"Thank you," I say, my voice barely above a whisper.

"One more thing." Mr. Russo leans forward again. "I know you didn't do anything wrong, but we're going to have to call your father. We have rules about bullying, and by law, I need to tell him."

"Do you have to?" I ask. "It's just that . . . he's really excited about living here and he seems to be trying for a fresh start. I don't want to ruin that."

"I'm afraid we do," Mr. Russo says. "But, Poppy, you didn't ruin anything. This isn't your fault."

Even though he's being so nice, Mr. Russo's words make me cry even harder.

"I'll tell you what," he says. "How about if we give it a week or so before I call your dad. To see if we can make some headway into who might have done this."

"That would be good, thank you."

Mr. Russo's phone buzzes. He picks it up, listens, and then says, "Send her in."

The door opens, and Britt comes shooting through it.

"Hello, Ms. Fuller," Mr. Russo says. "I understand you have something to tell me."

CHAPTER 13

"I DIDN'T DO IT." BRITT'S EYES ARE ANGRY SLITS THAT dart back and forth between Mr. Russo and me.

"Nobody said you did." Mr. Russo stands up and points to the chair next to mine. "Why don't you have a seat?"

"I don't feel like sitting." Britt looks at me. "You know I didn't do it, right, Poppy?"

I nod.

"Everyone out there is saying I did." She puts her hands on her hips.

"Why don't you take a seat?" Mr. Russo asks again, but it doesn't sound like a question this time.

Britt slumps into the chair, but she doesn't take her eyes off Mr. Russo.

"So." Mr. Russo starts pacing. "I know you were absent yesterday—"

"I wasn't feeling good," Britt interrupts.

"I know that. Your mother called. It was an excused absence." Mr. Russo sits on the edge of his desk. "But someone said they saw you near Poppy's locker yesterday afternoon, around dismissal."

"What?" Britt stands up. "That's impossible. I wasn't at school at all yesterday."

"Yes," Mr. Russo says. "We're just trying to sort all this out."

I close my eyes and lean back in my chair. Of course Britt couldn't have done it. She wasn't here all day, and she was home when I got off the bus with Brody. She was riding her bike. . . .

I snap my eyes open. She was riding her bike. I never asked her where she was coming from.

"Are you sure that you didn't stop by, Britt, to pick up homework?" Mr. Russo crosses his arms.

"I think I'd remember that," Britt says. "I told you. I wasn't feeling good."

If she was sick, why was Britt riding her bike? I try to remember what she said yesterday. Had she been sick, but then felt better? She seemed perfectly fine to me.

"Do you have any idea why someone would say they saw you if they didn't?" Mr. Russo asks.

"Of course." Britt is playing with the buckles on her leather jacket. "They're trying to frame me."

Mr. Russo purses his lips. "Why would they do that?"

Britt rolls her eyes. "Because they hate me."

"I'm sure nobody hates you—" Mr. Russo says.

"Do you actually remember being in middle school, Mr. Russo?"

A flash of understanding crosses Mr. Russo's face, and his gaze softens.

"Britt, you know I have to take anything anybody says very seriously. We're going to have to verify where you were yesterday."

"I told you," Britt says. "I was home. My mom knows that."

"Was she home with you?" Mr. Russo asks.

"She had to go to work."

Mr. Russo sighs. "Okay, Britt. Why don't you go back to class now?"

"Maybe you should be investigating whoever accused me of this." Britt stands up. "Maybe they're the person hiding something."

And with that, she storms out of the office.

Mr. Russo rubs his eyes. "So you don't think Britt had anything to do with this, Poppy?"

"I don't think so," I mumble. But then my mind goes back to yesterday afternoon. Why was she riding her bike if she was sick? And where was she coming from? If she did go to school at dismissal, the timing would have been perfect. She would have come home right around the time the bus got there.

I shake my head. It doesn't make sense. Britt wouldn't do that.

Would she?

"Why don't you let Mrs. Simmons know what textbooks need to be replaced from your locker, okay? We'll get those to you by the end of the day."

I nod.

"Think you're ready to head back to class?"

I nod again, even though I'm pretty sure I'll never be ready to head back to class. At least, not any class in this school. My eyes tear up again as I think about how much I miss Mandy.

As I walk down the unfamiliar hallway, I have to remind myself that I don't really know anyone here. Not Britt. Not Brody. Not even Kathryn.

I pass by my locker to find the janitorial staff still there, cleaning it up. The burning feeling I've had in my stomach all morning now moves up to my face. I feel so bad for them, having to clean up that disgusting mess.

It's the middle of first period by the time I get done with Mr. Russo, and everyone in science chuckles when I walk in the room. Kathryn gives me a frowny face until Mr. Walker looks away. Then she and Emily start their whisperfest. Brody smiles when he sees me, but I don't have the energy to smile back. I just want this day to be over with. I want it to be tomorrow already, so I don't have to step foot in this school.

The janitorial crew is done cleaning my locker by the time class ends, but I just can't bring myself to use it. Instead, I carry my backpack with me from class to class, careful to tuck it underneath my desk so nobody trips on it again.

I definitely can't bring myself to go to the cafeteria for lunch. Instead, I tuck myself into a corner of the library. I find some books on roses, and I spend the next forty-five minutes learning everything I can on tea roses and miniature roses and climbing roses. When the bell rings, my brain is so filled with flowers that I'm not sure I have any room left to learn anything else today.

I check the books out, shove them into my ever-expanding backpack, and make my way to my next class. The halls are crowded, and a couple of the eighth-grade boys are throwing a Nerf football back and forth. The ball comes *this close* to whacking me in the head, but I duck just as it swooshes past.

"Nice save, Poopy Poppy," one of them says, and the other one doubles over laughing.

I stare straight ahead and keep walking. When I get to language arts, I take my seat, pull *Tuck Everlasting* out of my backpack, and pretend to read until class starts.

I keep a low profile for the rest of the day. I stay in the classroom for as long as possible, then sprint to my next class, and do the same thing. The less time I spend in the hallway, the better.

The last bell rings, and I bolt out of class so I can snag the front seat on the bus. I'm so determined to get out of school that I barely notice the circle of kids yelling and jumping up to see what's going on.

Right in front of my locker.

Keep walking, I tell myself.

And as much as I want to, I just can't. I'm going to have to see sooner or later. I'm sure it has something to do with me.

I push through the excited students, until I'm close enough to see what everyone's so enthusiastic about. It's Britt.

She's got Kathryn pinned to the locker.

My locker.

I'm about to say something when Brody squeezes through the other side of the circle, which is now fifteen kids deep. He's out of breath and his hair is sticking straight up by the time he reaches his sister.

"What's going on?" Brody demands.

Kathryn's got tears streaming down her cheeks. "Brody, help me!"

"Britt, let her go," Brody says between clenched teeth.

"Stay out of this, Brody," Britt says. "This isn't any of your business."

"If it's your business, it's my business." I can barely hear Brody because he's trying to keep his voice down. "Mom would—"

"I'm sick of not doing the right thing because you think we have to protect Mom," Britt says.

"How is beating someone up the right thing?" Brody hisses.

"She's trying to frame me for what *she* did to Poppy's locker!" Britt's voice is getting louder.

"You don't know that," Brody whispers.

"Yeah, I do." Brit is yelling now.

I know I should say something. Do something. But my feet are paralyzed. This is happening too fast.

"Brody, please," Kathryn says. The smirk is gone from Kathryn's face, and it's replaced with a quivering lip and watery eyes. Even her ponytail is drooping.

Brody touches Britt's shoulder. "Let's go."

Britt shakes him off with one hand and holds on to Kathryn with the other.

"Go get a teacher," someone yells from the crowd.

"Britt, let's go." Brody stares straight at her. She looks at him for a few seconds, and I wonder if this is one of those psychic twin conversations I've read about.

Britt drops Kathryn, pushes through the crowd, and disappears.

Kathryn takes a deep breath, tightens her ponytail, and smiles at Brody. "Thanks for calling your dog off."

Brody winces but says nothing.

"You know I didn't do anything wrong, right, Brody?" Kathryn blinks her eyes a few times, and for the first time since meeting her I notice that her eyes are such a light shade of brown, they are almost yellow. Like a snake's.

"I don't know what's going on." Brody shakes his head.

"She just has something against me. You know that, right?" Blink. Blink.

"Yeah, she always has. But why?" Brody scratches his chin.

"I wish I knew. I've tried to be friends with her. But for some reason she hates me." Kathryn sticks her lower lip out, making her look like a five-year-old.

I don't realize that most of the other kids have left, and I'm one of the only other people still standing there.

Apparently, Brody and Kathryn don't notice either, because neither of them even looks my way.

I shake my head so that my hair is covering my face, and I slowly turn around. I keep my head down and walk as fast as I can to the bus, my overly stuffed backpack whacking me in the shoulder blades with every step I take.

I'm the first one on the bus, and I slide into my favorite seat, just behind the bus driver. This time, I'll make sure he stops at my house. I pull out *Tuck Everlasting* and stick my nose in it so nobody will talk to me. My plan doesn't work. A bunch of kids still greet me with "Hey, Poopy Poppy" as they make their way to their seats in the back.

I sink farther down into my seat and close my eyes. Just a few more minutes. A few more minutes until the weekend, and I won't have to deal with this insanity again for a while.

"Oh hey, Poopy." Kathryn sits down next to me, with Emily hovering over us. "Really sorry about what happened to your locker." Fake smile.

I ignore her and keep reading.

"Britt can be really harsh. You have to be careful around her."

I don't look up.

"And just so you know, trying to be friends with Britt

just to get closer to Brody won't work. He doesn't even like her. Nobody likes her."

I snap my head up. "I like her."

"I don't know why, after what she did to your locker." Kathryn winks at me and stands up. She and Emily giggle all the way to the back of the bus.

I can hear my own heartbeat in my ears, and I'm pretty sure my entire face is purple. If I wasn't completely sure before, I'm sure now. Britt didn't do this.

It was Kathryn.

I'm so angry that I don't notice that Brody's stopped at my seat.

"You okay?" he asks. "Your face is really red."

I pull at the collar of my shirt. "It's hot in here."

"Brody!" Kathryn calls from her seat. "Come sit with us!"

Brody looks up and waves. "Well, see you later, then."

"Yep." I don't even look up.

Once the bus starts moving, I remind the bus driver that I'll be going straight home today. When the bus stops in front of my house, I bolt down the steps and out the door before anyone can say anything.

I trudge down the driveway, but feel lighter with every step I take. It's the beginning of spring break. I can be normal for a whole week.

"Dad," I call as I hang my backpack up on the wall hook in the mudroom. "I'm home!"

"In the kitchen," Dad says. Something smells awesome, and I wonder if he's experimenting with new recipes again. I'm beginning to really like New Dad.

"What smells so—"

My Dad's wearing his REAL MEN COOK apron. And there's some woman standing next to him, holding a bag of kale.

"Hi, Poppy," Dad says, taking the bag of kale from the woman and putting it on the counter. "This is Mrs. Woodruff."

"*Griffin*-Woodruff," the lady corrects him, then walks over to me, sticking out her hand. "But you can call me Tammy."

"Uhhhhh, hi." I shake her hand. She smiles at me, but it's the kind of smile that only shows in her mouth and never reaches her eyes, which I notice, are the same color as a lizard's.

"This is Kathryn's mom," Dad says. "She's helping me with dinner."

"Oh." I shove my hands in the pocket of my jeans. "That's nice."

Tammy looks me up and down, and then tilts her head. "You look so much like your mother."

"What?" It comes out as a whisper.

"Oh, your mother and I were good friends when we were kids."

"You—you were?" I stammer.

"Oh yes, she was lovely." She gives me another smile—the kind that doesn't quite reach her lizard eyes.

And then it hits me.

Tammy Griffin-Woodruff.

Tammy Griffin.

Tammy.

This is the Tammy from Mom's letters.

The one who made Mom miserable.

CHAPTER 14

"WELL," DAD SAYS. "WITH TAMMY'S HELP, WE SHOULD have quite the amazing dinner tonight."

"She's not staying, is she?" Ugh. Did I just say that out loud? Dad does a double take, apparently as surprised as I am that I said that out loud.

"I mean, uhhhhh, is she staying for dinner? Tonight?" I give my best fake smile.

"Not tonight." Dad smiles at Tammy, sufficiently satisfied with my cover-up. "We ran into each other at the grocery store. When I mentioned that I've been cooking, Tammy offered to help teach me a few things."

"Careful she didn't sneak some cow pies in there," I say under my breath.

"What was that?" Dad asks.

I clear my throat. "I said, hopefully she'll sneak some good pies in there."

"Oh, I have some great pie recipes." Tammy beams.

I nod. "I'll bet."

"I have a great idea," Tammy says. "Why don't I bring some over next weekend? Maybe Saturday night?"

"Saturday night?" My voice sounds much higher than normal.

"That's perfect!" I swear Dad is floating at least three inches off the floor. "Why don't you bring Kathryn with you to dinner?"

A gurgling noise comes from somewhere deep in my chest, and I start to cough. And cough.

"You okay, Poppy?" Dad asks.

"Yeah." I pat my chest in between coughs. "Fine."

"That's so nice of you to invite her, David," Tammy says. David? Who calls my dad David? Everyone calls him Dave. "But she'll be at her dad's next weekend."

I cough again.

"She'll be so sorry to miss the opportunity to spend some time with you, Poppy." Tammy's lower lip juts out in the same pouty-face style as Kathryn's. I try to fake a smile, but my mouth only twitches.

Tammy packs her cooking supplies into a pink-and-green quilted paisley cooler bag.

"Let me help you with that," Dad says.

"Thank you, David." Tammy touches Dad's hand.

I think I might throw up.

"I'll walk you out," Dad says.

"It was so wonderful to meet you, Poppy. You're every bit as lovely as Kathryn said you were." Tammy's lizard eyes stare at me, and I can't help but think she's going to stick a pointed tongue out next. "I'll see you next week."

"See you next week," I mumble, and then she follows Dad to the front door. Apparently Tammy's too good to use the side door like the rest of us.

I sit down at the kitchen table, trying to take in what just happened.

Is Tammy, Mom's biggest arch nemesis, Dad's new girlfriend?

If so, Dad's in even bigger trouble than I am.

Tammy is a big, fat liar, just like her daughter is. Tammy was not Mom's friend when they were my age. She was her enemy. I have to let Dad know, but how? I can't tell him about the letters. What if he takes them away from me? I can't risk not having them—not having Mom—in my life.

I hear the front door open, and Dad floats back into the kitchen. He sits down in the chair next to mine.

"You okay?" he asks.

I shrug.

"I'm sorry. I didn't expect that Tammy would still be here when you got home from school. Guess we lost track of time." Dad plays with his wedding ring, which he still wears after all these years.

I don't say anything.

"That's not how I wanted you to meet her. I wanted you to have more time to get used to the idea of, you know, me dating."

"It's not that," I say. "Even though that is pretty gross."

Dad laughs. "Then what's bothering you?"

"It's just that . . ." I take a deep breath. "I don't think Kathryn is as nice as she seems."

Dad frowns. "Why do you say that?"

"She just . . . she seems kinda fake. And what if her mom's fake too?"

"Well." Dad leans back in his chair. "I think it takes some time to get to know people. So that's what we have to do. Let's get to know them. Both of them."

"I'm not sure I want to get to know Kathryn any better, Dad."

"It's only been a few days, Poppy."

His tone of voice tells me the conversation is over. At least I know there's still a little bit of Old Dad left.

* * *

I spend the week of spring break reading about roses. It rains almost every day, so there's not much I can do but read about them. Not that I'd know what to do even if it was sunny outside, but I know I have to do something. After five days with my nose in the books, I decide I need to be more proactive.

I find the EVMS directory in the drawer next to the phone in the kitchen. I pull it out and page through it until I get to the *F*s." I find the number I'm looking for, take a deep breath, and dial.

Ring. Ring. Maybe nobody's home. *Ring.*

"Hello?" I'm about to hang up when I hear a voice on the other end of the line.

"Hi. Brody?"

"Yeah."

"Oh, hey. It's Poppy." I swallow hard.

"Hey, Poppy. How's your spring break going?"

"Pretty quiet. You?"

"Same."

"So, uhhhh." I start pacing in the kitchen. "I was wondering. Remember when I was at your house and you and Britt said you might be able to help me start my garden?"

"Yeah."

"Would you guys maybe want to come over tomorrow?" I hold my breath.

"Oh, we can't tomorrow."

"Oh." I feel like I was punched in the stomach, and all the air is forced out of my lungs. "That's okay. I know you're really busy and—"

"How about Saturday?"

"Saturday?"

"Yeah," Brody says. "We can come over on Saturday. We have dentist appointments tomorrow."

"Really?" I can breathe again. "That's great. I mean, it's not great that you have to go to the dentist, but—"

Brody laughs.

"So, then, I'll see you guys on Saturday."

"See you then."

I hang up and do a happy dance around the kitchen. I twirl over to the window that faces the backyard and look outside. Soon, roses will be blooming by the boatload.

And I don't care what anyone says. I know that Mom will make sure they're ready for the 4-H fair.

CHAPTER 15

EVEN THOUGH I DIDN'T SET MY ALARM, I GET UP RIGHT before six thirty. It's just getting light out, and I stumble over to my dresser and pull out the next letter. I bring it back to bed with me, crawl under the covers, and open it.

A piece of paper comes tumbling out, landing on my bed. I pick it up. It's a movie ticket stub. I hold it in my hand while I start reading.

May 4, 1985

Dear Poppy,

What a roller-coaster week! Where to begin?! I guess I'll start at the beginning . . .

I went back to the library to look for THE CARE AND KEEPING OF ROSES when I ran into Brian at the checkout counter! He noticed I was holding a gardening book, so we got to talking. I told him my leaves were looking yellow, and he asked me if I'd tested the soil. I hadn't, so he offered to come over to help. He said he owed me one after I helped him find the Abe Lincoln book.

So yesterday, Brian came over, and as it turns out . . . my soil was too alkaline. Who knew? Brian knew, that's who!

After we added garden sulfur to the soil, he asked me if I wanted to go see THE BREAKFAST CLUB, which is playing at the Dollar Theatre in Winslow. Mom agreed to drive, and Brian and I went ON A DATE!!!!!!!! We didn't hold hands or anything, but it was just the two of us and a big bucket of popcorn. Oh, THE BREAKFAST CLUB was soooooooo good. It's about a bunch of kids who would never get to meet if it weren't for a Saturday-morning detention, and they all find out they have more in common than they think. Kind of like Brian and me! I didn't even know he knew anything about gardening until we started talking, but it turns out his Mom's a big gardener.

So that was the up part of the roller coaster. Now comes the downside. . . .

Tammy found out that Brian helped me with my roses, and she'll never let me hear the end of it. She told me that even if I win the 4-H fair, it won't count, because I didn't do the work myself. And then, to make things even worse, "someone" (I'm sure it was Tammy!!!!) took my brand-new Reeboks out of my locker just before gym and smeared dog poop all over the soles. So of course, when I put them on, I unknowingly tracked dog poop all through the locker room and out into the gym. Mrs. Kahill FREAKED OUT. She made all of us check our shoes and when she learned it was me, she screamed at me in front of the entire class. It was SOOOOOOO embarrassing. Tammy and Kelly just laughed and laughed.

Of course I can't prove it was them, but who else would do something like that? I know for sure there wasn't dog poop on my shoes when I put them in my locker. They were brand-new! I'd never even worn them before!

So between this, and all of the other reasons that I'm sure you already know, I definitely have to beat Tammy in the 4-H fair. Someone's got to show her that she can't be the biggest scuzzball of the universe and get away with it.

Just a few more weeks till the fair . . . when Tammy will be kicked off her throne (or is it thorn? hee hee) of roses!

Until next week.

Love & friendship always & forever,
Daphne

I read the letter again, just to be sure it said what I think it said.

Yep.

Dog poop.

Now I know, without a shadow of a doubt, that Kathryn is the one who put the cow manure in the locker. That family has a penchant for poop.

But now I have to find a way to prove it. And I have to find a way to warn my dad.

I grab my notebook and pen and start writing.

Dear Mom,

Okay, now I'm really freaked out.

But I think I know why you're telling me this. You know it was Tammy who pulled the poop prank on you, just like I know it was Kathryn who pulled the poop prank on me. You're trying to warn me, aren't you?

Don't worry. I got the message loud and clear. I'll find a way to prove that both Tammy and Kathryn aren't who they pretend to be. And I'll get Dad to see it too.

I can't believe Brian helped you with your roses, because Brody is coming over today to help me start my rose garden! Well, Britt and Brody. But still! The garden will be in the exact same place yours was, and the roses will be awesome! With your help, I'll bet they might even be ready for the 4-H fair, even though everyone tells me roses don't grow that fast. But most people don't have their Mom's spirit to help speed things up. . . .

Speaking of Brody, I don't understand why he can't see how Kathryn really is. Britt sure knows it.

Also speaking of Brody (and I just realized as I'm writing this), Brian helped you with your garden and Brody's helping me with mine . . . and Brian and Brody both start with the letter B!

I'm not sure what you're orchestrating from up there, but I'm so happy we're going through this together.

I never heard of THE BREAKFAST CLUB, but it sounds cool. Maybe I'll see if I can find it on Netflix.

Love ya,
Poppy

PS: Dad's been cooking lately. Did you know Dad even knew how to cook?!

I put the letters away, get dressed, and slowly open my bedroom door. I'm the only one awake, which means I have the house to myself. This reminds me of the city days. I'd spend hours alone, and I'm surprised to find that I don't really miss that time.

I go downstairs to the kitchen and pull out the books on roses that I took out of the library. After about an hour of leafing through them, I pour myself a bowl of cereal. I'm not sure if New Dad cooks breakfast during spring break.

Dad stumbles into the kitchen at around ten a.m.

"Good morning, Poppy." He yawns. "Did you eat?"

"Yep. Hours ago."

"That's good." Dad gets the coffee going. "Is Troy up?"

"Not yet."

"Whatcha reading?" Dad sits down next to me and the kitchen starts to smell like coffee.

I show him the book cover. "So you're really serious about this gardening stuff, huh?"

"Yes." I sit up taller. "I am."

"You know, Tammy's quite the gardener. Maybe she can help—"

"That's okay." I interrupt him. "I've got friends coming over tomorrow to help."

"Oh, that's good." Dad nods, but his smile fades, and he

looks a little bummed that I don't want help from Tammy.

Dad gets up to pour his coffee, and I go back to my rose books. My head hurts from trying to decide if I want to grow my roses from seeds or cuttings, or if I want to plant them in containers first or straight into the ground. I close the book and rub my eyes, wondering if Mom had these same problems.

The next morning, I get up extra early to clean my room. I have no idea if Britt and Brody are even going to see my room, but I want to be prepared.

I'm leafing through my flower books when I hear the crunching of gravel on the driveway through the open window. I peek out the side door and see Britt and Brody lean their bicycles against the garage.

"My friends are here," I call out to Dad as I put my sneakers on.

I step out the side door, and immediately feel the sun on my face. I squint. It's the first real springlike day we've had since I got here.

"Hi, guys." I wave to Britt and Brody. Britt's wearing a black T-shirt, but there's no sign of the black bandanna.

"Hey," Brody says. "Can we leave our bikes here?"

"Sure." I walk over to the garage. "How long did it take you to ride here?"

Britt shrugs. "Not long. Our mom's working today, and anyway, it's nice out."

"I haven't been here in a long time." Brody looks around and points to the field on the other side of the house. "That's where the raspberries used to be."

"Yeah." I can actually feel the little seeds between my teeth, and my mouth waters. "Maybe someday they'll be there again."

Brody smiles. "Really? Your parents going to start the farm up again?"

"Well, my dad wants to learn to farm." I kick a big stone from the driveway. "But like me, he has a long way to go."

"What about your mom?" Brody asks.

"Oh, I thought you knew." I look down at the ground. "My mom died."

"Oh, wow," Brody says. "I'm really sorry."

"It was a long time ago," I say. "Five years, actually. I just thought you knew, you know, since you knew my grandparents."

"It's probably been that long since we were here," Brody says.

"Longer," Britt chimes in. "We weren't even in school yet."

Brody nods. "Yeah, that's right."

"So." Britt puts her hands on her hips. "Let's get this

farm back in action." She smiles, and it's amazing how different she looks when she does. She looks so much like Brody when she smiles.

"This is where my dad said the garden can go." I point to the dusty, brown patch of land, which was once thriving and alive with color.

Britt pushes the bangs out of her eyes and stares at the would-be garden. She bends down and picks up a blob of dirt. She feels it in between her fingers as if it were a piece of silk. Then she looks up at the sky, looks down at the dirt, and looks up at the sky again.

"This will do," she says finally.

"Great!" I smile. "There are tools in the shed. We can—"

"Hang on," Britt says. "We're going to need some top-soil. And some compost."

I blink.

"I don't know if we have any of that." But then again, I don't even know what any of that is. "I'll go ask my dad."

I run into the house and find Dad vacuuming the family room. I had no idea Dad even knew how to use a vacuum. Back in our apartment, Troy and I had to keep our rooms neat, and a cleaning lady came in once a week to clean the rest of the place.

"Oh hey, Poppy." Dad turns the vacuum cleaner off. "What's going on?"

"Do we have topsoil or compost?" I hope I remembered that right.

"I just ordered some topsoil. It was delivered yesterday. I had them drop it off behind the barn. No compost, though. That we have to make ourselves."

"Can we do that now?"

Dad laughs. "No. That takes some time. Compost is basically rotting organic matter. You know, fruit, vegetables, leaves that break down after a while."

I crinkle up my nose. "Sounds smelly."

Dad smiles. "Not if it's done right."

"So can I use some of the topsoil for my garden?"

"Sure. There's a wheelbarrow and some shovels back there too."

I head to the door when Dad calls me back. "Please don't leave your phone on the kitchen table. Remember we're having guests tonight."

"Fine." I stuff the phone in my back pocket, then run back outside and tell Britt and Brody about the topsoil behind the barn. Britt sends Brody and me over with the wheelbarrow, while she goes into the barn to search for a hoe. Which, apparently, isn't just something Santa Claus says.

"Hey," Brody says, handing me a shovel. "If it makes you feel any better, I don't have a dad."

"You don't?" I take the shovel from Brody.

"Well, I do, but I don't see him anymore."

"That stinks," I say.

Brody shrugs. "He's kind of a jerk."

"I'm really sorry." I look at Brody, but he's looking at the topsoil. "But maybe he'll change. People can change."

Brody smiles, but it's not his usual light-up-his-face smile. It's kind of a halfway smile, and he almost looks sad. "Maybe."

"Well." I try to catch his eyes but he's still focusing on the topsoil. "Thanks for telling me."

"Yeah," Brody says. "Since you told me about your mom, you know, I wanted to tell you that not everybody has two parents, so I kind of know how you feel."

If my knees weren't wobbling so much and I could actually move my legs, I'd run and give Brody a hug.

"I really appreciate that," I say instead. He doesn't say anything for a few minutes, so I figure he doesn't want to talk about it anymore. I pick up my shovel and take a deep breath. "Okay, let's do this."

Brody laughs.

"What's so funny?"

"You are." He leans against his shovel, smiling at me. "You're—you're not like anyone else around here."

I feel like I just ate a spoonful of compost. I can't believe Brody thinks of me like an outsider too. Just because I—

"I mean that in a good way." Brody elbows me in the side.

"You do?"

"Yeah." Brody isn't looking at the topsoil anymore. He's staring *right at me*, and the sunlight is making his green eyes glow so brightly that they look neon. "I like you. I mean—you're cool."

I'm pretty sure my head is about to explode, and I want to tell him that he's cool, and that I like him too, but I'm afraid if I try to say something fire will come out of my mouth instead of words.

After I don't say anything for a few seconds, Brody looks down. "I guess we should start filling the wheelbarrow or Britt will have us working overtime."

I nod, and we both dig into the big mound of dirt with our shovels. It doesn't take long to fill the wheelbarrow, and Brody pushes it over to the garden, me tagging behind.

We dump the dirt out, and Britt spreads it across the designated garden area. We do this for another couple of hours, and when we're done, I can't believe what I see.

There's a garden. I mean, there are no flowers or anything in it yet, but Britt found some wood in the barn and made a cute little fence along the outside to keep animals out.

After the last of the dirt is spread, Britt looks up, wipes her sweaty forehead with a gloved hand, and says, "Now the real fun begins."

Britt goes over to her bike and opens up what looks like a small cooler that's strapped in behind her seat. Unlike Tammy's lavish cooler, Britt's is old and worn. She brings the cooler over to the garden and sets it on the ground.

She lifts off the lid and pulls out a tiny little rosebush. There must be at least half a dozen of them in there, each planted in a miniature pot.

"Awwww," I say. "They're so cute."

"They're babies," Britt says. "And like babies, they need lots of love and care to grow."

Britt strokes the tiny leaves as if they were the ears of a puppy. As she holds the roses, everything about her is different. Her eyes soften, her shoulders relax. She has none of that tough-girl exterior that I saw the first day of school.

"First, we have to dig a hole for each of them," Britt says, and Brody hands me my shovel. "So let's mark the spots where each of them will go."

Britt makes six little Xs with a stick, all in a row. Brody and I each take three, and we start digging the holes while Britt gently removes the roses from their pots.

Once the holes are dug, Britt gently holds the rosebush toward me. "Here you go. Your first baby!" Her green eyes light up like fireflies.

I hold my hands out, not quite sure what I'm supposed to do with this teeny, very delicate plant. If I hold too tightly, I'll squeeze it to death. If I hold too loosely, I'll drop it. Britt can probably sense my extreme newbie-ness, so she drops the plant into my palms and tells me to just cup my hands around it.

"Now just place it into this hole." She's standing over the first hole in the row.

I bend down, holding the plant as if it were made of fine china, and place it in its new home.

"Perfect." Britt nods. "Next, we need to pack the soil gently around it."

Brody kneels beside me and we each push the soil toward the tiny plant. Our hands accidentally touch, and I practically fall backward.

"Sorry." He gives me a real quick smile, then looks back down at the dirt.

"Oh, it's okay." I put my head closer to the ground so he can't see that my face is turning more red than any rose has ever been in any garden anywhere in the whole wide world.

"Nice." Britt nods, satisfied with our technique. "Now you just want to do the same for the rest of them."

Brody and I repeat the process five more times, and when we're done, there are six tiny rose plants sticking out of the ground. Just knowing that these roses are in the exact same spot as my mom's roses were when she was my exact same age makes me feel lighter than I've felt in days.

"We've got to get a picture of this." I pull my phone out of my pocket and get pictures of each and every rosebush. Then Britt, Brody, and I huddle together to take a selfie with the garden in the background.

"Now, just for fun," Britt says, and she pulls a packet out of her cooler. "Let's throw some seeds in there."

Britt tells me to hold out my hand, and she pours something that looks like little pebbles into my palm. Then she gives some to Brody.

"It's really hard to plant roses from seed, but since we have some extra space, I thought we could give it a try."

We sprinkle the seeds down into the soil. Britt stands back and admires her handiwork. "We should cover them in mulch." Britt looks at me. "Does your dad have any?"

"I'll go ask." Just as I'm about to turn around and go inside I hear my stomach rumble. I have no idea what time it is, but it is probably well past lunch. "You guys want to come in and get something to eat?"

They both nod enthusiastically, then take their gardening gloves off and put them on their bike handlebars. We kick our muddy shoes off, and they follow me into the kitchen. Troy's in the family room playing video games, and Dad is nowhere to be found.

"That's my brother, Troy." I point to the blob on the couch. "Troy, this is Britt and Brody."

Troy waves, but he doesn't take his eyes off the television.

"Have a seat." I wave over to the kitchen table, and then go into the pantry for some chips and salsa. I grab the lemonade out of the fridge and pull some mint leaves out of the produce drawer. I open the bag of mint leaves and take a nice, long whiff.

Smells like Mom.

"Let's eat on the front porch." I pour three glasses of lemonade and plop a mint leaf into each. I put the glasses, chips, and salsa on a carrying tray I find in one of the top cupboards, and carefully lift the tray off the table.

"I can help with that," Brody says, and takes the tray from my hands.

"Want me to carry anything?" Britt asks.

"I think we're all set," I say. "Let's go out the front door."

We step out onto the porch, and Brody sets the tray down on the table in between the rocking chairs. He picks up a glass and takes a sip of lemonade.

"This is delicious." He licks his lips. "The mint makes it even more awesome."

I smile. "Mint was my mom's favorite."

"Mint's my favorite too," Brody says. "Especially when it's fresh."

We spend the next few minutes slurping our lemonade and crunching on chips. We're quiet, but it's not that awkward quiet that people get when they don't know what to say to each other. It's more like that quiet people get when they don't need to explain every little thought that goes through their heads.

The front door opens and Dad steps out with a broom.

"Hi, there." Dad gives us a wave. "Don't mind me, guys. Just going to tidy up a little bit."

Of course he decides to clean RIGHT NOW.

"Oh hi, Dad." I put my lemonade glass back down on the tray. Dad keeps sweeping the same spot over and over again, looking up at me every few seconds. I think he's waiting for an introduction. "These are my friends Britt and Brody."

Brody stands up and extends his hand. "Hello, Mr. Pickler."

"Hello, Brody." Dad shakes his hand. "Nice to meet you."

Britt gives a little wave. "Hello, sir."

"Hi there, Britt." Dad squints as he looks at her, and then his eyes go back to Brody. "Are you guys twins?"

"Yes, sir." Brody nods.

"You look so much alike." Dad smiles, and starts sweeping the porch.

"Can I help you with that, sir?" Brody asks.

"No, thank you, Brody," Dad says. "This will only take me a minute."

"Did you see the garden?" I ask Dad.

He stops sweeping. "No, I haven't been back there yet. How's it looking?"

"Great." I dip a chip in salsa. "These guys have been a huge help."

"Fantastic," Dad says. "Maybe they can help me get the rest of the farm up and running."

"We're happy to help anytime." Brody's voice sounds deeper than usual, and I wonder if he's making it sound that way on purpose.

"Thank you, Brody. Maybe you're looking for a summer job?"

"Really?" Brody's eyes grow huge. "That would be awesome."

Dad pats Brody on the back. "Great! You're hired. How about you, Britt?"

"Maybe, sir," Britt says. "I usually help my mom with stuff around the house in the summer."

Dad nods. "She's lucky to have you."

"Remember, Poppy." Dad looks at me. "We're having a guest for dinner. So if you could start cleaning up, that would be nice."

I roll my eyes when he turns to Britt and Brody.

"You kids want to stay?" he asks.

"Thank you, sir," Brody says. "But we told our mom we'd be home for dinner."

"Another time, then." Dad winks.

"Thank you, sir," Brody says again. None of my friends back home ever called my dad "sir."

Dad goes back inside and I groan. It's so totally embarrassing when your dad tries to be cool around your friends.

"What?" Brody asks. "Your dad seems really nice."

I shrug. "He's okay—now. He was very different before we moved here. I hardly ever saw him."

"We hardly ever see our mom." Brody takes a chip and shoves the whole thing in his mouth. "She's always working."

"That's how it was with my dad," I say. "But now that

we're here he doesn't have to work as much, so he has more time to . . . I guess to be a dad."

"It must be nice to have him back," Brody says.

"Yeah." I hold the glass of lemonade in my hands and stare down at the mint leaf floating inside. "But I miss my mom."

"I miss my mom too," Britt says, her voice barely above a whisper.

I want to ask her why, since she sees her mom every day, but she's looking down at her feet, and I get the feeling that maybe she doesn't want to talk about it any further. Instead, I raise my lemonade glass. "Here's to moms."

Britt and Brody raise their glasses to mine, and they make a light *clink*ing sound as they touch.

"Speaking of moms, you'll never guess who my dad is having over to dinner tonight."

Britt and Brody look at each other and shrug.

"Kathryn Woodruff's mom."

Britt stands up, and lemonade splashes out of her cup. "Your dad is dating Tammy Woodruff?"

"They're not exactly dating." My voice is so loud it echoes off the porch floor. "They're just—she's just coming over for dinner."

"Mmmm-hmmm," Britt says. "She's trouble."

"You hardly even know her, Britt." Brody takes a swig

of lemonade. "How do you know what she's like?"

"Because Mom hates her," Britt says. "And I'm sure she has her reasons."

"You don't know that." Brody shakes his head.

"What are her reasons?" I lean forward in my chair and look at Britt.

Britt shrugs. "I don't know. But whenever we see her at school events, or at the grocery store, my mom says words she shouldn't and turns the other way."

"Do you think maybe you can get the scoop from your mom?" I say. "I need to get some concrete evidence so I can convince my dad not to see her."

Britt and Brody look at each other for a split second.

"Our mom—she's—she's been really busy and stuff. We try not to bother her with too much unless it's an emergency." Brody takes an ice cube out of his lemonade and starts chewing on it.

I look back and forth between Britt and Brody, but neither of them looks up at me.

Don't they know that this *is* an emergency?

CHAPTER 16

GOOD GOBLINS. MY FATHER IS WEARING A TIE.

He's also running around the house like getting ready for dinner is an Olympic event. There's something in the oven (looks bad, smells good), there are candles on the table (looks good, smells bad), and hold on a second . . . *Did Dad gel his hair?*

"Poppy, can you set the table?"

I stare at him. "Dad, it's only three o'clock."

"And that means Tammy's going to be here in an hour. I want everything to be ready before she walks in the door."

I roll my eyes and head for the cabinet where we keep the dishes.

"Not those," Dad says. "The good plates."

I blink. "What good plates?"

"The ones in the china cabinet in the dining room." Dad slips his hand into a giant oven mitt and grabs a steaming dish out of the oven.

I just stare at him. After a few seconds of taking things out and putting things into the oven, he realizes I haven't moved.

"Poppy? The dishes?"

"Those are Grandmom's good dishes." I put my hands on my hips.

Dad closes the oven door, then looks back at me. "You know they're ours now."

"And we're using them for the first time on Tammy?" My fists clench, and I dig my fingernails into my palms to distract me from the fact that tears are sprouting in my eyes. "We're supposed to use them for special occasions only."

Dad adjusts his apron. "Having someone over for dinner is a special occasion."

"You just met her. Shouldn't we save the good china for family and friends?" He opens his mouth to say something, but I keep going. "I mean, friends you've known for longer than five minutes."

Dad takes a deep breath. I know I sound like a bratty five-year-old. But I'm still right. Tammy doesn't deserve my grandmother's—my mother's mother's—best china.

"Fine," Dad says tightly. "Use the regular dishes."

I can't tell if Dad sees my point of view, or if he just doesn't have time to argue with me. I grab four dinner plates out of the cabinet and set each one on the place mats dad set out. The place mats are flowery and fancy, but since I don't recognize them as ours—or Grandmom's—I don't say anything. I bet Dad went out and bought new place mats. Old Dad used to eat off paper plates.

When the table is set, and Dad is satisfied with whatever he's got in the oven, he calls Troy in from outside, and tells us both to take a seat at the table (reminding us, of course, not to touch anything).

"So, kids." Dad pulls out a chair and sits down. "Tammy should be here soon."

"Okay?" Troy says, like he has no idea what Dad's new girlfriend has to do with him. Boys can be so clueless.

"I just want to make sure you're . . ." Dad fiddles with his apron strings. "You know, that you're okay with it and on your best behavior."

I laugh. I can't help it.

"What's so funny?"

"On our best behavior? Dad, I think that boat sailed like five years ago. Nobody says that to kids who are our age."

"Well." Dad's cheeks turn pink. "You know what I mean."

"Yeah, that's cool." Troy fidgets in his chair. "Anything else? I need to finish washing the truck."

"Go," Dad says. "And hurry up so you can get cleaned up and dressed in time for dinner."

"But I am dressed." Troy looks down at his ripped jeans and beat-up *SpongeBob* T-shirt that he's had since fifth grade.

"Yeah, not quite, buddy." Dad pulls at Troy's shirt. "Please put on some clean clothes. And it would be great if they've been washed sometime this century."

Troy grumbles as he goes outside, but I don't get up.

Dad's tapping his fingers on the side of his chair. "Dinner will be fun. You'll see."

"Mmmm-hmmm."

"Tammy seems really nice, Poppy. Try to get to know her, okay?"

I sit up straighter in my chair. "Okay, Dad. But you've got to make the same promise."

Dad looks at me, tilting his head like a dog trying to decipher human language.

"You have to try to get to know her too," I repeat. "Just because someone seems nice, doesn't mean they *are* nice."

Dad nods. "Fair enough."

"Okay, then." I stand up. "It's a deal."

"Poppy?" Dad looks up at me.

"Yeah?"

"Thanks. For trying, I mean."

My chest feels like it's being squeezed into a parka that's three sizes too small. But then I remind myself that the sooner Dad learns the truth about Tammy, the better it will be for all of us.

Just as I'm about to go upstairs to text Mandy, the doorbell rings. Dad jumps up off the chair, rubs his hands together, and gives me a brilliant smile.

"Ready?"

I nod.

Bring it on, Tammy Griffin-Woodruff.

CHAPTER 17

I SAY HELLO TO TAMMY (BECAUSE DAD MAKES ME), then go upstairs until dinnertime. I eyeball my underwear drawer every two minutes. Wouldn't Mom understand if I read her next letter a little early? Don't dire times call for dire measures?

I flop down on my bed and put the pillow over my face. I promised I'd open one a week, so that's what I'll do. Even if it kills me.

I open my nightstand drawer and pull out Mom's pictures. I place them gently on the lacy bedspread, and spread them out so they're side by side. There's Mom with her cowboy boots. Mom with her big hair. Mom's scraggly roses.

I hear Dad's booming laugh coming from the kitchen,

and the taste in my mouth reminds me of that time I ate moldy sour cream. Do I actually have to go down there?

I get my answer five minutes later, when Dad calls us for dinner.

My stomach grumbles as I trudge down the steps. As much as I'm dreading this dinner, apparently my stomach is looking forward to it. Stupid stomach.

"Hi there, Poppy." Tammy's hair is not in a ponytail. "It's so nice to see you again."

"You too," I mumble.

"Kathryn was so disappointed that she couldn't join us tonight."

I purse my lips together and force them to turn upright into something that resembles a smile.

Troy comes leaping down the stairs. He's dressed in a pair of (clean) jeans and a short-sleeved polo shirt. Like Dad, he has some kind of weird gel stuff in his hair, which makes him look a little like an unattractive porcupine.

Tammy compliments him on his 'do. And his shirt. And his eyes.

My goodness, David. He has the same beautiful blue eyes you have.

Troy is eating it up. He actually believes her! This just proves what I've known all along. Troy is full of shenanigans.

"What can I help you with?" Tammy turns to Dad when she's done inflating Troy's ego.

"Nothing at all." Dad gestures for the table. "Won't you all sit down? Dinner is served."

I'm about to sit in my regular seat when Tammy slides right in there like she's been sitting in it for years. Good thing I catch myself before I sit right on her lap.

"Oh, is this your seat?" Tammy notices that I'm hovering, and starts to stand up.

"No, no. Stay there." Dad brings a big salad bowl and puts it on the table. "Poppy can sit across from you."

So I do.

"Oh, David," Tammy says as Dad sits down. "This looks wonderful."

"I hope so." Dad unfolds his napkin and puts it on his lap. "Please, dig in!"

I serve myself some salad, which turns out to be the most amazing thing made with the best lettuce that I've ever had. The dressing is warm, and it's made with walnuts, goat cheese, and dried cranberries. I have two helpings.

Next, Dad brings out a pan of roasted chicken breast, smothered in caramelized onions and mushrooms. It's to die for. As happy I am to eat this amazing meal, I can't help but feel angry that Dad's been holding out on us. We've been living on pizza delivery and Chinese takeout for the last five years, when he could cook like this?

"So Poppy." Tammy takes a dainty bite of chicken. "How do you like EVMS so far?"

I shrug. "It's fine."

"Are the kids nice?"

"Some of them." I emphasize the word "some," but she seems unfazed.

"Well, Kathryn tells me that she loves having you there. She thinks it's wonderful to have a bright new face in the group."

"That's nice of her," I say. Tammy doesn't sense the sarcasm.

"It's terrific that everyone's so welcoming," Dad chimes in.

It's obvious to me now that neither of them know about the Poopy Poppy incident. I guess Mr. Russo hasn't told Dad yet.

"Your dad tells me you've been working on a garden." Tammy blots the corner of her mouth with her napkin.

"Yep." I take another serving of chicken.

"You know, your mom and I used to garden together."

I stop chewing and look at her.

She laughs. "Of course, we were more like opponents than partners!"

I swallow. "You were?"

"Oh, sure. Our roses were always competing for

the blue ribbon at the 4-H fair." Tammy smiles at the memory.

"Who won?" My voice is low and raspy.

"You know"—Tammy puts her fork down—"I don't even remember. It was silly anyway. To let that kind of stuff get in the way of the friendship we had. Luckily, our many years of being best friends overshadowed that childish competitiveness."

Mom and Tammy were best friends? But that's—that's impossible. I read Mom's letters. There's no way that could have been true.

Unless . . .

Unless those letters were written before Mom and Tammy became friends. Maybe they just had a rough start, like Britt and me.

"Is it okay if I talk about her?" Tammy asks Dad. He gives a half smile and nods.

"You know, Poppy . . ." Tammy looks me in the eyes, and suddenly instead of snake eyes, Tammy's eyes look like the color of caramel, all warm and gooey. "You can ask me anything about her."

"I can?"

"Sure." Tammy reaches across the table and touches my hand. "There's no reason that her memory shouldn't be alive and well in your life."

Then she drops my hand and says, "Now, who's ready for pie?"

Dad clears the dinner dishes. I know I should help, but I'm too stunned to move. Could it be that I had it all wrong about Tammy? Mom's letters, just like the photos inside them, are just a snapshot of her life. Maybe later letters and photos would tell a very different story.

Tammy cuts the cherry pie and gives me the biggest slice.

It's the best pie I've ever tasted.

CHAPTER 18

EVEN THOUGH THERE'S A POSSIBILITY THAT TAMMY isn't as bad as I thought she was, Kathryn still terrifies me.

I climb the stairs to the bus on Monday morning, and my stomach sinks when I see that someone is sitting in the seat behind the bus driver. Brody notices and waves me over. Of course, he's in his usual seat in front of Kathryn and Emily.

I take a deep breath. Maybe Kathryn will be nicer, now that her mom and my dad are . . . whatever they are.

I smile at Kathryn as I'm about to sit down, but as usual, she just glares back at me. I guess nothing's changed.

"How was the big date?" Brody whispers to me.

"Okay," I whisper back.

"Have you been watering the roses?"

"Every day."

Brody smiles. "Good."

I keep waiting for Kathryn to kick the seat, or pull my hair, or shout out *POOPY POPPY* to the whole bus. But she doesn't. She just ignores me.

When we get to school, Brody walks with me to our lockers. I worry that maybe Kathryn's ignoring me because she did something far, far worse than putting cow poop in my locker, but when I get there, everything's fine.

Kathryn doesn't talk to me in any of my morning classes. She doesn't even look at me.

Things are going so well that I decide to brave the cafeteria for lunch. I sit at my usual table, and Britt joins me. Kathryn and her ponytailed posse stay at their own table. Nobody bothers us.

"Do you think it's the calm before the storm?" I ask Britt, in between bites of lasagna.

"What do you mean?" Britt takes a chocolate chip cookie out of a Ziploc bag.

I glance quickly at Kathryn's table. "She's been so quiet."

Britt shrugs. "Who knows with her. Maybe she found someone else to pick on."

"Or maybe her mom told her to leave me alone," I say under my breath.

"Oh yeah!" Britt puts her half-eaten cookie on a napkin. "How was the dinner date?"

"You know . . ." I lean back in my chair. "It wasn't that bad. Tammy was actually pretty nice."

"Really?" Britt's eyebrows shoot up. "That's a surprise."

"I thought so too."

"It's not like I know her that well," Britt says. "Kathryn and I don't ever hang out together. But my mom definitely doesn't like her, and my mom likes everybody."

I stare at Britt for a minute. She always gets a sad look on her face when talking about her mom.

"Are you and your mom close?"

Britt looks down at her cookie. "We were. Before my dad left."

"Yeah, I get it. My dad and I were close before my mom died too. Then he just sort of . . ." I search my mind for the right word. "Disappeared."

"My mom just got really busy. And stressed out. I still try to talk to her about stuff, but Brody always stops me. He says she doesn't need any more on her plate."

"That stinks," I say.

"Yeah." Britt takes a bite of her cookie.

We finish our lunch in silence, and bring our trays back up to the counter.

"What do you have next?" I ask Britt.

"Woodworking." Britt puts her silverware in the big blue bin. "How about you?"

"Intro to Agriculture." We walk out of the cafeteria. "Why don't you take that class? You'd love it."

"Because I'd have to enter into the 4-H fair, and I'm not going to do that." Britt stops at her locker and I wait while she gets her books out.

"So? You'd rock the 4-H fair. You'd beat everyone." And then I add, "You'd beat Kathryn."

Britt closes her locker and we make our way down the hallway toward mine.

"I don't think flowers should be grown for the purpose of winning or losing," Britt says. "Something about that just feels wrong to me."

I don't understand what she's talking about, but I don't push her. I guess it will just be up to me to beat Kathryn. Me and Mom, that is.

Kathryn's already in Intro to Agriculture by the time I get there. She and Emily are standing over Brody's desk, giggling. I take my usual seat next to Brody.

"Hey, Poppy," he says.

"Hi." And then I look up at Kathryn and Emily and say hello to them as well, but they don't even acknowledge my presence. Oh well. Being ignored is much better than being harassed.

Mrs. Quinn starts the class like she usually does. She tells everyone to start working on their 4-H projects.

"Poppy." Mrs. Quinn waves me over to her desk. "Have you chosen a project yet?" Mrs. Quinn folds her hands and looks up at me, as if I'm about to present her with the most spectacular 4-H project in the history of 4-H projects.

"I, uhhhh," I begin. "I haven't exactly chosen anything yet. But I have a few ideas."

"Well," Mrs. Quinn says. "What's in the running?"

I glance back at Kathryn to be sure she's not listening to me. She's not. "I'd like to grow roses."

"Excellent!" Mrs. Quinn claps her hands together.

I smile.

"How long have you been growing roses?" Mrs. Quinn asks.

I pause. "I started recently." I don't tell her "recently" means last week.

"And you think they'll be ready in time for the fair?"

"I think so." I don't tell her that my dead mother is helping me. I have a feeling that wouldn't go over so well.

"Wonderful! I can't wait to see what blossoms for you." She chuckles at her own pun.

I go back to my desk and pull out my book on roses. Brody walks over to me. He's holding a roll of chicken wire.

"What did you decide?" He taps the chicken wire roll on my arm.

"I decided to grow roses."

"What?" Brody sits down in his chair and leans toward me. "You know they're not going to be mature in time."

"They might be." I give him a hopeful look.

"Poppy, there's no way—"

"I know you think that, Brody. But these roses are . . . special."

"Special? They're not special. They came from our garden, so unless you know something I don't, you could fail this class."

I lean forward so that the tops of our heads are almost touching, and then I lower my voice. "Maybe I do know something you don't."

The bell rings, and I give him a little wink as I head to my next class.

CHAPTER 19

DAYS GO BY WITH ABSOLUTELY NO DRAMA FROM Kathryn. I even sit with Brody on the bus, and she doesn't say a word.

As I walk into school on Thursday, Mr. Russo calls me into his office.

"Have a seat, Poppy." I do, and he sits on his desk across from me. "It seems we've found out who vandalized your locker."

"You did?" I lean forward in my chair. I wonder what kind of trouble Kathryn's going to get into.

"Yes, the student will be suspended, and a formal apology will be given."

Maybe that's why Kathryn's been so quiet.

There's a knock on Mr. Russo's door, and Mr. Russo

stands up. "Ahhh, here's the apology now."

I can't wait to see the look on Kathryn's face when she—

But it's not Kathryn.

It's Thomas. The kid who tripped over my backpack the first day of school.

"Have a seat, Mr. Palmetto."

Thomas sits next to me. "Don't you have something to say to Poppy?"

Thomas looks down at his hands. "I'm sorry, Poppy."

I just stare at him. I hardly even know Thomas. Why would he do that to me? He can't still be upset about the backpack, can he?

"Thank you, Thomas. Now please go wait in the main office. Your parents will be here soon."

Thomas plods out of Mr. Russo's office, closing the door behind him.

"Are you sure it was Thomas?" I ask Mr. Russo, once Thomas is out of the room.

"Quite." Mr. Russo nods. "He posted a picture of your locker—filled with manure—on his Instagram account. Plus, he lives on a dairy farm. So it all makes sense."

"But why? What does Thomas have against me?"

"I don't think it was personal, Poppy. Thomas has a history of pranks. This was probably just a game to him."

"So are you going to tell my dad?"

"Yes, now that our investigation is complete. But I'll explain to him that you're perfectly safe here, and that Thomas pulled an extremely inappropriate practical joke."

At least I won't have to tell my dad that his new girlfriend's daughter pooped my locker. And it's a good thing, too. When I get off the bus, I see Tammy's car in the driveway. She and Dad are sitting on the front porch.

"Hi, Poppy," Dad says. "How was school?"

"Fine." I walk up the steps of the porch and put my backpack near the front door.

"Tammy made lemonade. Would you like some?"

Tammy holds the pitcher out to me, and I notice there are no fresh mint leaves inside.

"No, thanks." I pick my backpack up again.

"So," Dad says. "Mr. Russo called."

"Yeah?" I adjust my backpack onto my shoulders.

"He told me what happened to your locker."

"Yeah. It was pretty gross."

"Are you okay?" Dad asks.

"I'm fine," I say, sounding as laid-back as possible. "The school had to give me new textbooks, though."

"I've known Thomas Palmetto for a long time," Tammy interjects. "This doesn't surprise me at all."

"Really?" I look at Tammy.

"Unfortunately so." She nods. "He's constantly looking for the wrong kind of attention. I'm really sorry you had to be a recipient of that."

"Thanks." I take my backpack off again and drop it by the door, then turn to leave. "I'm going to check on my roses."

"Mind if I come with you?" Tammy puts the pitcher back on the table.

I glance over at Dad. He looks like someone just gave him a brand-new car.

"I don't mind," I say, because what am I supposed to say?

Tammy and I walk around the house to the backyard. I unroll the hose from the side of the barn and gently water the rosebushes. While they're still pretty small, they are definitely growing.

"These are beauties." Tammy bends down to get a closer look.

"Thanks," I say.

"You know . . ." Tammy stands up. "If you ever need any help, I'm only a phone call away."

I study her face. I've read that you can tell someone's lying if they don't blink while looking at you. Tammy blinks.

"Do you think . . ." I shuffle my feet. "When do you think these roses will mature?"

Tammy looks down at the flower. "I think they'll be amazing by next spring. In fact, I'll bet you give Kathryn a run for her money at the 4-H fair next year." She smiles.

"What about this year?"

Tammy purses her lips. I can't tell if she's thinking, or if she's trying not to laugh. "Definitely not this year. They're too young."

I nod, but I don't agree with her. I know Mom will work her magic.

"Thanks for showing these to me, Poppy." Tammy smiles.

"Sure," I say. And even though Tammy's being super nice to me, I feel a teensy bit guilty about standing here talking to her. Even though she says she and Mom were BFFs, Mom's letters say the exact opposite.

And the last thing I want to do is betray my mom.

CHAPTER 20

I GROPE FOR MY PHONE IN THE DARK. IT'S FIVE A.M. on Friday. There's no way I can go back to sleep when I know today's a letter day.

I shuffle to my underwear drawer and pull out the metal box. Once again I bring the box to my bed and crawl under the covers. I turn on the flashlight app on my cell phone, and read the next letter.

May 11, 1985

Dear Poppy,

What an amazing week this has been! I only wish you were here with me.

Dear Poppy

Brian asked me to the square dance next week. Of course I said yes! I don't think Tammy knows, because she hasn't done anything awful to me yet.

The garden looks fantastic. I've been spending lots of time in there, making sure the soil is right. I guess it's working, because my roses never looked so good. Even my dad noticed! He was so proud that he took a photo of the roses, which I've included for you to see.

I really think I'm going to win this year, Poppy. And I know I'll do it honestly. Unlike Tammy. We both know that she uses her mom's roses. I just wish we could prove it. Oh well. Karma will get her someday! And let's hope that "someday" is at the 4-H fair!

Until next week.

Love & friendship always & forever,

Daphne

I reach my hand inside the envelope and pull out the photo of the roses. I gasp. They're beautiful. They hardly resemble the photo from just a few weeks ago. Mom did it! I'll bet anything she beats Tammy at the fair. Maybe that's exactly what happened. Maybe Mom beat Tammy, and then Tammy apologized and they became BFFs. That would make sense. I reach for my pen and notebook to write Mom back.

Dear Mom,

I had a great week too! My roses are looking good, and I've sat next to Brody every day on the bus.

Even Kathryn isn't being mean to me. As it turns out, she didn't put that cow poop in my locker. Some kid named Thomas did. I guess he's a big joker or something. Which makes me wonder . . .

Maybe Kathryn isn't as bad as I thought. And maybe Tammy turned out to be not as bad as you thought. Tammy's been over a couple of times now. I hate to say it, but she seems kind of nice.

Maybe it just takes a while to get to know people.

Anyway, I'm super excited about the fair. Can't wait to see what you'll do with the roses!

Love ya,
Poppy

PS: Has anyone ever called Dad "David"?

I put the letters away and crawl back into bed. It's too early to get up. Instead, I flip through the photos of Britt, Brody, and me from last weekend. I text one of the pictures to Mandy. She's dying to see what Brody looks like.

I sit next to Brody on the bus, and once again, Kathryn says nothing. In fact, it's another normal day. Maybe Tammy put in a good word for me.

I water my garden as soon as I get home, and spend most of the afternoon just staring at it. I feel closer to Mom when I'm out here, almost like she's out here too. I stay outside until Dad calls me in for dinner (creamy risotto with mushroom and peas!). I go to sleep with a smile on my face.

The next morning, my stomach tells me it's time to get out of bed and grab breakfast. Although New Dad is an amazing cook, on the weekend he's more of a brunch kind of guy. I guess now that he can sleep in on weekends, he does.

I grab a cereal bowl out of the cabinet and pour some weird-looking brown flakes into it. New Dad doesn't buy sugary cereals. I'm about to sit down when I happen to glance out the window.

I press my nose against the glass to get a better look. I can't believe what I'm seeing.

My hands fly up to my mouth and my bowl drops to the floor with a clank, little brown flakes and milk spilling out onto the wood. I don't even bother to put shoes on. I run out the mudroom door and to the garden.

My roses are destroyed.

Something—or someone—trampled all over them. Some are ripped out of the ground. The little red buds looked like smooshed cherries, hardly recognizable as flowers.

I fall to the ground and sob.

My flowers—Mom's flowers—are ruined.

Dad comes running outside. His hair is sticking straight up and he's in his slippers.

"Poppy," he huffs. "What happened?! I heard a crash and then I heard you scream and there's a broken bowl on the kitchen floor and . . ."

He stops when he sees the garden.

"What—what happened?"

I open my mouth to speak, but the words won't come out. Dad bends down beside me and rubs my back. At least New Dad is much better with crying children than Old Dad was.

"My—" *Sob.* "Roses are—" *Sob.* "Gone!" *Sob. Sob. Sob.*

"Oh honey, I'm so sorry."

"How could this have happened?" *Sob.*

Dad stands up. "I don't know. Maybe an animal got in here."

"But there's a fence." *Sob. Sob.*

"It's a low fence. Something could have jumped it."

"What kind of animal jumps fences?"

"I don't know, Poppy. I'm still learning about this farming stuff myself." Dad reaches out his hand. "How about we go inside for some tea?"

I shake my head no.

"Poppy, you can't stay out here forever."

"You go. I'll be in soon."

Dad sighs and turns to leave. "I'll boil the water so the tea will be ready when you are."

From my seat in the dirt, I spot a tiny flower that somehow survived the attack. I reach for it and hold it in my palm. It's so small, but it's perfect.

I'm going to have to replant everything and build a

bigger fence. I have to be sure that whatever animal did this won't ever come back.

I know there's no point sitting out here any longer. As much as I try, I can't make sense of this. Why would Mom bring me to plant this garden, only to have it ruined within a week?

As I stand to leave, I notice something odd in the far corner of the garden. I walk over there, my feet sinking into the soil. I bend down to get a closer look.

It's a footprint.

But it's not my footprint, although it could be. It's around the same size.

But this is a footprint with treads, and I don't own shoes with those kind of treads.

So unless some sort of flower-eating animal wears size-seven shoes, it was a person who destroyed my garden.

CHAPTER 21

THE TEAPOT IS READY ON THE STOVE, BUT I GUESS DAD couldn't wait. He went back to sleep. But, I noticed, he cleaned up the mess I made in the kitchen first.

I run upstairs and grab my phone. It's still early—not even eight—but I text Britt and Brody anyway to tell them what happened. To my surprise, Brody texts right back.

Brody: B right over.

I throw on a pair of jeans and a T-shirt. I don't even bother brushing my hair, although I do brush my teeth. I'm not *that* irresponsible.

I have no appetite anymore, but I figure I should eat something. I grab a banana and eat it by the kitchen window so I can stare out at the dirt pile that was once my garden.

There's a knock on the door, and I open it to find Britt and Brody standing there, mouths hanging open.

"I can't believe this," Britt says, shaking her head. Her whole face is drooping.

"I'll show you the footprint." This time, I slip on a pair of old flip-flops before going outside.

I point out the footprint to the twins. Brody studies it closely. "Yep, that's a shoe print all right."

Britt is looking at the flowers. "Poppy, there's no way an animal did this."

"Because of the footprint?"

"And because if it was an animal, chances are it would have actually eaten the roses. Or at least chewed on them. But nothing here looks chewed on. It just looks like the plants were pulled out of the ground and trampled."

I stare at her.

"This was most definitely a person," Britt says finally.

"But why?" I blink back the tears that are threatening to spring from my eyes.

"Do you think Thomas would do this?" Britt asks.

"No way," Brody says. "His mom grounded him for life after the locker incident."

"Maybe he snuck out at night?" I ask.

"I don't think so. He lives too far away to walk or bike here. And anyway," Brody says as he points to the footprint, "this print is way too small to be Thomas's. Have you seen his feet? He wears like a size fourteen."

Britt bends down and touches the footprint. "It looks like a girl's shoe."

I bend down next to her. She's totally right. The print is too slender and small for someone like Thomas.

"I'll bet it was Kathryn." Britt stands up and crosses her arms.

"But Kathryn's been better lately," I say.

Britt raises an eyebrow at me. "'Better' meaning she just ignores us?"

"That *is* better," I mumble.

Brody doesn't say anything. He's still investigating the footprint.

"Whoever did this won't get what they want." Britt stomps her foot in the dirt. "We're going to rebuild."

"But how?" I shake my head.

"The same way we did it the first time," Britt says. "I'm going to ride back home, get some more rosebushes, and we're going to plant them."

"But what if someone just comes back and destroys them again?" I stare at the torn-up rosebushes and swallow hard.

"Then we'll keep planting new ones. Whoever did this can't keep it up. They'll get caught eventually." Britt says this with such certainty that there's no point in arguing with her. And anyway, she's right. Whoever did this won't win.

Britt gives Brody and me instructions on how to get the trudged-up soil ready for planting again, then she hops on her bike and speeds down the driveway.

I start to pick up the ruined plants and put them in a pile on the grass. All I can picture in my mind is Mom's sad face. Sad that I failed her and couldn't do the one and only thing she wanted me to do: grow roses and win the blue ribbon.

I squeeze my eyes shut to make the image go away.

"Are you okay?" Brody asks.

I open my eyes and realize I'm just standing there with my eyes shut tightly. I must look ridiculous.

"Oh yeah," I say. "Just . . . The sun was in my eyes."

Brody nods. "Well, I brought you something. You know, to make you feel better."

"You did?"

"Yeah." He digs into the back pocket of his jeans and pulls out an iPod.

"You got me an iPod?"

"No." Brody laughs. "I mean, not to keep. But I want you to borrow it."

I blink.

"Whenever I feel bad about something," Brody begins, "I listen to this playlist. It's awesome and upbeat, and it always makes me feel better."

He holds the iPod out and I take it, turning it over in my hands.

"Wow," I say. "That's really nice of you."

Brody shrugs, and his cheeks turn red. "Keep it for as long as you want."

"Thanks." I stare down at the iPod, and then back at Brody.

Brody smiles and then goes back to cleaning up the garden. I join him, and we have it all ready for planting by the time Britt comes back with the rosebushes.

It takes most of the day, but we get the new rosebushes in the ground.

Britt stands back and smiles at her handiwork. "Yep, these look great."

"Maybe we need to booby-trap the garden." Brody looks at Britt. "Got any ideas?"

Britt purses her lips. "We could try barbed wire."

"Then how would we get in and out?" Brody asks.

"We could build a gate. With a lock."

"Won't that take a long time?" I ask. I don't know anything about building gates, but it sounds like a lot of work.

"Maybe we can work on it next weekend," Britt says.

"What about until then?" I ask.

"Have you thought about getting a dog?" Brody replies.

"Troy's allergic." Stupid Troy.

Nobody has any better ideas, so we go inside for some snacks and lemonade. We're getting the lemonade out of the fridge when Dad comes downstairs. This time, he's wearing a tie *and* a jacket.

"Why are you all fancy?" He smells like pine trees.

"Tammy and I are going out tonight. There are plenty of leftovers if your friends want to stay for dinner."

Britt and Brody look at each other. The secret twin conversation again.

"Sure," Brody says. "Thank you. We just have to leave before it gets dark."

After lounging around on the porch for a while, we heat up some leftovers and eat them in the family room in front of the TV. Britt turns on HGTV and sits down on the floor. Brody sits next to me on the couch.

The sun is just starting to set after dinner, so I walk the twins outside to their bikes.

"The third song is my favorite," Brody says before he rides off.

I pull the iPod out of my pocket and put the headphones

in even before I'm back in the house. I plop down on the couch and listen.

Brody was right. The songs do instantly make me feel better. I forward to the third song. I've never heard it before, but the iPod's screen reads "The Power of Love" by Huey Lewis and the News.

It's a catchy tune. I whip out my phone and Google it.

The release date is 1985.

Omigod. Mom even has control over Brody's iPod! This thought makes me even more sad about the flowers.

"I promise," I whisper to Mom. "I'll take care of the roses and make you proud, okay?"

I listen so hard that I can actually hear dust floating around the room, but Mom doesn't answer.

CHAPTER 22

BRODY IS WAITING FOR ME WHEN I GET ON THE BUS on Monday morning. I smile as I sit down, and I hold out his iPod.

"Thanks for this," I say. "You're right. The songs are awesome. Especially number three."

"Yeah." Brody smiles. "That's my mom's favorite. She used to play that album all the time."

"I'd never heard it before, but I loved it."

"I have an idea." Brody takes the headphones, puts one bud in his ear, and hands me the other one.

We listen to Huey Lewis and the News all the way to school.

Once again, Kathryn and company ignore me. I like

the ignoring much better than I like the bullying. I do wonder what's going to happen if Dad and Tammy get serious. Will she ignore me in front of them, too?

I'm still thinking about this at lunch. I never thought about having a stepmom before.

"Does your mom ever go on dates?" I look at Britt, who's slurping a Capri Sun.

"Yuck. No."

"How long has it been since your dad left?"

"About two years." She crumples the empty Capri Sun pouch in her hand. "I don't think she'd date anyone again unless he was Superman. She was really upset when my dad left."

"I hope my dad doesn't marry Tammy." I sigh.

"Then Kathryn would be your stepsister."

We both make a sour-lemon face at the exact same time and laugh.

The rest of the week goes smoothly. I check on my roses every day after school, and every day they look better and better. I'm pretty sure Mom's working her magic.

On Friday morning, I hop out of bed and grab the next letter out of the box. I sit at my desk chair and read.

May 18, 1985

Dear Poppy,

The square dance was AMAZING! Brian came and picked me up, and of course Mom and Dad took tons of pics (one included), which was totally embarrassing. Brian even had a rose for me! I pressed it into my A POPULAR GUIDE TO ROSES book. When Brian was here, he took a peek at my roses. Even he said they look great! He said I must be taking good care of them. Which you know I am.

Tammy still gives me the evil eye every minute of the day, but other than that, she doesn't come near me. I'm beginning to think that maybe she's just given up. Maybe she sees that torturing me isn't working. Then again, you never know with Tammy. . . .

Until next week.

Love & friendship always & forever,
Daphne

There's a photo of Mom and Brian included in the envelope. Mom has that huge Mom smile (and that huge Mom hair), and she's holding the rose that Brian gave her. She's wearing a floral-print dress with a denim jacket over it. Either Mom had huge shoulders, or her jacket has some serious shoulder pads. Either way, she looks like she's glowing. I hold the photo close to my chest for a minute, then pull out my notebook so I can write her back.

Dear Mom,

You and Brian looked so cute! And it was so nice of him to give you a rose. I really hope you're right about Tammy. I hope she's realized that bullying you won't work. Maybe that's how you become friends. Maybe after you win the blue ribbon, she apologizes and all is forgiven.

I hope so, because that means there's hope for Kathryn and me to become friends. If Dad's going to date her mom (sorry), then we certainly can't be enemies.

I've been hanging out a lot with Britt and Brody. You'd really like them. They're both excellent gardeners and they're both nice to me. Britt and I didn't start out as friends, and look at us now.

I can't wait to hear if that's what happened with you and Tammy.

Love ya,
Poppy

PS: I really like the outfit you wore for the square dance. Very country chic.

Dad's already in the kitchen by the time I get there. He's cooking French toast with apples and cinnamon. I drool a little.

"Good morning, sweetie."

"Hi, Dad. Smells good."

"Almost finished." Dad flips a piece of French toast in the pan. "Oh, I found a bunch of books in the attic that I thought you'd like. I put them on the kitchen table."

Piled in the middle of the table are books on gardening. There's *The Gardener's Encyclopedia*, *Great Gardens*, and *A Popular Guide to Roses*.

Wait.

A Popular Guide to Roses. Wasn't that the book Mom mentioned in her letter?

I quickly grab the book by the spine and shake it out.

"Easy there, Poppy." Dad looks up from the French toast. "Those books are about the same age as your old man, you know."

Sure enough, a dried rose falls out of one of the pages. I look at it for a second, then put it back before Dad can see.

"Thanks, Dad." I grab the books and run up to my room. "I'm going to put these on my shelf."

"Okay, but come right back down," Dad yells after me. "Breakfast is almost ready."

I neatly stack the books on my bookshelf, and gently take the rose out of *A Popular Guide to Roses*. I hold it in my palm. It's browning on the ends, but otherwise it's held up pretty well. I bring the flower up to my nose. There's still the tiniest hint of fragrance, almost like a memory. I pull the metal box out of my underwear drawer and add the rose to it. Then I go downstairs for some of New Dad's French toast.

At breakfast, Dad tells us that Tammy's coming over for dinner again. And this time she's bringing Kathryn.

CHAPTER 23

LUCKILY, I'M STILL UPSTAIRS WHEN TAMMY AND KATHRYN arrive. I hear Dad gushing over how much he's heard about Kathryn, and how helpful it was that Kathryn showed me around school the first day, blah, blah, blah. Dad calls me down in a singsongy voice.

"Poppeeeeeeeeee. Tammy and Kathryn are heeeeeeeere."

I make my way into the kitchen, where Tammy is *ooh*ing and *aah*ing over whatever Dad has on the stove. Kathryn's standing next to Tammy, but she's not saying much.

The first thing Tammy does when she sees me is give me a breath-squeezing hug.

"Oh, Poppy." Tammy makes her frowny face. "Your father told me what happened to your roses. I'm so sorry."

I politely remove myself from her grip, and step back. "It's okay. I've replanted."

Tammy's frowny face gets frownier. "You did?"

"Yes." I smile. "The garden looks even better than before."

"Well." Tammy's frown turns upside down. "I'm so happy for you. Kathryn, isn't that great news?"

"That's great news." Kathryn is standing behind Tammy. Her voice sounds genuine, but her smile is pure fake Kathryn.

"You sure got that done quickly," Tammy says. "What's your secret?"

I glance over her shoulder at Kathryn. Before I could answer, Dad chimes in.

"Poppy had some friends over to help."

Why does Dad have to pick now to be so involved in my life?

"That's wonderful." Tammy looks back at Kathryn. "Anyone we know?"

"Those Fuller kids," Dad says. "The twins."

Tammy's face looks like someone stung her with a Taser. "Britt and Brody?"

"Nice kids, those two." Dad adds some spices to the pot.

"Well, David . . ." Tammy tucks her hair behind her ears. "Brody is fine, but you really need to watch out for Britt."

Dad stops stirring. "Why?"

"She's trouble."

I'm just about to open my mouth and defend Britt when Dad steps in.

"She's been good to Poppy."

"Okay." Tammy shakes her head. "Don't tell me later that I didn't try to warn you."

The room falls silent until Troy comes barreling down the stairs.

"Smells great. When's dinner?"

I've never been so happy to see Troy in all my life.

"We have a few more minutes until the spices merge to perfection," Dad says. "Poppy, why don't you go show Kathryn your garden?"

"Yes, Poppy." Kathryn looks like a cat who's cornered a mouse. "I'd love to see your garden."

The thought of showing Kathryn my garden—Mom's garden—makes my stomach churn. But Dad and Tammy are looking at us like we just told them we got into Princeton, so I lead Kathryn outside.

"Here it is," I mumble, and point to the line of itty-bitty rosebushes growing out of the ground.

Kathryn snickers.

"What?" I know I should ignore her, but I just can't. Not when it comes to this.

"There's no way these will be ready for the fair." Kathryn crosses her arms. Her fingernails are painted red.

"Maybe not," I say. Even though I know they will be.

"Why do you even bother?" She doesn't say it in a mean way, but more like she's really wondering.

"What do you mean?" I ask.

"You never grew roses before you moved here. These will never be ready in time. And I win the blue ribbon. Every year. So I just want to know. What's the big deal with roses?"

"You should know," I answer. "You grow them."

Kathryn snorts. "I only grow them for my mother."

I think I gasp a little. But before I can tell Kathryn that's exactly why I grow them too, she goes on.

"My mother makes me. I swear she'd kill me if I didn't win the blue ribbon." She picks at her nail polish.

"I'm sure that's not true. I'm sure—"

"Trust me," Kathryn interrupts. "You don't know my mother."

Kathryn's lower lip starts to quiver the tiniest bit, and I actually feel bad for her. But just as quickly, I also wonder if this is another one of her tricks meant to manipulate me. If I feel sorry for her, then I won't enter the fair, and she'll win as usual.

Dad opens the windows and yells out, "Girls. Dinner's ready."

Kathryn turns to walk inside before I can even say anything more.

Dad outdoes himself at dinner. Eggplant parmesan with homemade marinara sauce, pasta al dente, and homemade cannoli for dessert. I have no idea where Dad learned to make cannoli. The dinner conversation consists of mostly how good dinner was, which is fine with me. We don't talk about school. We don't talk about flowers, and we don't talk about Britt or Brody.

Kathryn gives me a weak smile when it's time for them to leave, and, for the first time since I met her, I sort of feel sorry for her. I come *this close* to actually giving her a hug good-bye.

I feel the exact same way toward her all week at school. She's still not talking to me, but she's not glaring at me either. I call that progress.

Britt and Brody come over every day to help with the garden. I don't tell them what Tammy said about them. Sure, Britt doesn't finish her homework, and is always late for class, and skips school way more than she should, but she's amazing with flowers. And she's a good friend.

I wake up late on Friday, so I have no time to read Mom's next letter. I spend all day thinking about it, but Britt and Brody come over right after school to work on the garden, so by the time I'm alone in my room, it's bedtime.

Finally! I open the box and pull out the next letter. I wonder where Mom's hidden the next stack. Or, maybe she—or her ghost—is just going to come talk with me directly. Seeing her again, even if it is in spirit form, would be way better than letters.

This envelope is different than the others. It's padded, and when I pull the letter out, I see why. Mom included one of those old-fashioned tapes—I think it's called a cassette—in the envelope. There's also a class picture, and I pick out Mom immediately. She's the one with the brightest smile.

May 25, 1985

Dear Poppy,

The strangest thing happened last night. Dad said he heard noises outside in the middle of the night, so he went to check things out. Someone was in my garden! Dad chased them away, and he said it was too dark to see who it was, but thank goodness he was sleeping with the windows open and heard something. We looked around this morning, and everything looked okay, except for this one rosebush that was trampled.

I'm sure it was Tammy. Who else would want to hurt my flowers? Especially a week before the fair?!

I'm totally paranoid to sleep now. What if she comes back to finish the job? I want to sleep in a sleeping bag outside, but my parents won't let me.

Everything had been going so well, too. Tammy's been pretty mellow at school. And Brian gave me the best mix tape ever! It even has "The Power of Love" on it. How did he know that's my favorite?

One more week til the fair. Oh, how I wish you were here. Hey! That rhymes (sort of)!

Until next week (THE FAIR!!!!).

Love & friendship always & forever,
Daphne

I drop the letter on the floor.

No. Way.

Somebody tried to ruin her garden, just like somebody tried to ruin mine?

And "The Power of Love" was Mom's favorite song? It was on Brian's mix tape *and* Brody's iPod? My heart is about to pound out of my chest and fall to the floor next to the letter.

Things are really happening now.

CHAPTER 24

EVERY MORNING BEFORE SCHOOL FOR THE NEXT FEW weeks, I check on my flowers. And every morning they look a tiny bit better. But not nearly good enough.

As we get closer to the fair, I start to get super nervous.

"They're not going to be ready in time for the fair," I say to Britt at lunch one day.

"No, they're not." She hands me a potato chip. "The fair is in two days. But you knew that, Poppy. It would take a miracle for roses to mature that fast."

I swallow both the potato chip and the lump in my throat. A miracle is exactly what I'm counting on.

There's still time. But just in case, I talk to Mrs. Quinn at the end of Intro to Agriculture.

"My roses," I begin, "may not be quite ready by Saturday."

"Oh no, are you having pest problems?" The lines in Mrs. Quinn's forehead wrinkle.

"Something like that," I say. "Would it . . . If I had to, can I change my project?"

"It's a little late, I'm afraid." Mrs. Quinn taps her pencil on her chin. "But I'll tell you what. Why don't you take a look at this list and see if perhaps you already have something you can put together? Just in case."

Mrs. Quinn hands me a list of project ideas, and I smile at her. "Just in case."

I practically leap off the bus and straight to my garden after school. I'm fully expecting to see mature, blooming roses, the prettiest ones ever.

But I don't.

They look exactly the same as they did this morning.

I sit at the kitchen table and pull the sheet Mrs. Quinn gave me out of my backpack. I scan the list for just-in-case ideas.

Photography, woodworking, sewing, global education, composting. There's no way I can do a project about any of these things in two days.

And then something catches my eye.

"Yes!" I jump up off the kitchen chair, run up the stairs, and get started on my backup project.

Just in case.

* * *

I wake up on Friday morning, throw the covers off me, and go to grab Mom's last letter. I pull the envelope out and in big red letters it says, POSTFAIR LETTER! What does that mean? Do I have to wait until after the fair to read it? Or did she write it after the fair? My thoughts swirl around in my head. I'm dying to read it now, but what if Mom is trying to tell me that I have to wait? Spirits are so vague.

Just in case, I slip the letter back inside my drawer. I guess I can wait one more day.

Maybe she found another way to send me a message today.

Maybe . . .

I have to get to the garden. I fly down the stairs and bolt out the side door.

My heart sinks into my toes when I step outside. My roses haven't changed. Not even a little bit.

I sit down on the grass, my back against the barn.

"There's still one more day," I whisper to myself.

I drag myself inside and get ready for school. Brody can tell something's wrong the minute I get on the bus.

"What happened to you?"

"My roses still aren't ready."

Brody gives me a little shove. "Of course not. You knew they wouldn't be."

I don't answer him.

"Poppy?" Brody nudges me again. "You did know they wouldn't be, right?"

"It's okay," I say, avoiding his question. "I did a just-in-case project last night. I think it's really good."

"What is it?" Brody's smiling. He loves this 4-H stuff.

"It's a surprise," I tell him. "Maybe you'll see it tomorrow." Or maybe not, because I'll get my miracle roses.

Kathryn's absent today, and Britt mentions that she's absent the day before the fair every year. Apparently, it takes her a long time to prepare. This, of course, makes me more nervous. Even if my roses blossom overnight, will I have time to "prepare?"

After school I sprint to the garden.

There's no change.

"Come on, Mom." I say. "We only have one more day. We can do this."

CHAPTER 25

I WAKE UP TO DAD SHAKING ME BY THE SHOULDERS.

"Poppy. Poppy. It's time to get up. We're going to be late."

I open my eyes and bolt upright. "Is it Saturday?"

"Yes," Dad says. "We overslept. We've got to go."

I push Dad aside and fly down the steps. I don't even bother to put shoes on as I fling open the side door and run out to the garden.

My mouth hangs open when I see it.

My roses look exactly the same.

Tears pour from my eyes. I don't understand. I thought this was the deal. Our deal. I'd plant the garden, and Mom would be sure the flowers were ready for the fair.

But no, there are no flowers.

I must have done something wrong somehow.

I failed Mom.

Mom. Today's fair day! Today's the day I read her last letter.

Dad peeks his head out the kitchen window. "Poppy, what are you doing out there? You've got to get dressed and get your project into the truck. We have to be out of here in three minutes."

I run back inside and tuck Mom's last letter into the back pocket of my jeans so I can read it the minute the fair ends.

I throw my poster board in the truck (I tell Dad it's on plant genetics), and Dad and I eat granola bars in silence.

We pull into the packed fair parking lot—which is just a giant muddy field—and find a spot at least half a mile from the entrance. I decide to leave my poster board in the truck rather than lug it around with me to the flower exhibit. I can come back for it later.

We plod across the mucky terrain until we enter the gates of the fair. A man wearing a plaid shirt gives us a program. Dad opens it up and searches for the flower exhibit. We still have to be there to support Kathryn.

"Looks like it's in Barn A," Dad says.

I look up at all the buildings and tents. I have no idea where Barn A is, and I don't care. I can't believe that my roses aren't ready. Why would Mom put me through this and then not come through with the roses?

I kick a rock off the path, and it rolls to a wooden sign with arrows going every which way. One of the arrows says, BARN A. I follow it and, sure enough, Barn A is right next to us.

I look at Dad, who's intently studying the map in the program. I should probably just tell him that Barn A is directly to our left, but the later I am for the exhibit, the better. Maybe we'll even miss the ribbon ceremony, which Kathryn is guaranteed to win.

Dad holds the program up and turns his body in the opposite direction. "It says we are here, so Barn A must be—"

I can't stand it anymore. "It's over there." I point to our left.

"So it is." Dad rolls the program up and puts it in his back pocket.

We head over to the barn. I trudge behind Dad. Even though Kathryn's not the *total* monster I thought she was, I still don't want to see her win the blue ribbon.

Dad and I walk into the barn, and Tammy waves us over to the front of the exhibit. I have to admit—the flowers are spectacular. Tammy and Kathryn are standing next to the table with the roses. Tammy gives Dad a peck on the cheek (ewwww) and smiles at me.

Kathryn gives me a tiny wave.

"Hi." I force a smile. "Good luck."

"Kathryn's going for her fourth consecutive blue ribbon." Tammy bounces up and down on her toes. "If we win this, she'll beat the record for most consecutive ribbons in her age category. And you know who currently holds that record?"

Dad and I shrug.

"I do!" Tammy says, beaming.

Kathryn just looks at the floor.

"So." Dad gestures to the flowers exhibited on the tables. "Which one of these beauties is yours?"

"I'm number thirty-two." Kathryn points to a vibrant red rose standing proudly in a clear vase. The flower is bigger and brighter than the other roses. She'll win for sure.

My shoulders slump. That should have been my rose. Mom's rose.

"Last call for entries." The voice comes over a loud speaker. "All exhibits must be ready for judging by nine a.m."

Tammy's talking a mile a minute, telling us all about what it takes to have champion roses. Kathryn just nods along, because after all, she would know.

"Three minutes." The loudspeaker booms. "Three minutes to have all entries checked in."

As riveting as Tammy is (NOT), my attention is drawn to someone running into the barn at full speed. My jaw drops to my socks when I see who it is.

It's Britt.

And she's holding something close to her chest. As she gets closer I see that it's a clear vase.

And towering over the top is the most perfect pink rose I've ever seen.

Dad, Tammy, and Kathryn follow my gaze.

"What is she doing here?" Tammy demands, hands firmly on her hips.

"I don't believe this," Kathryn mutters. But she doesn't say it like she's upset. More like she's impressed.

Britt places her vase on the exhibit table with the other roses. She attaches a card with the number fifty-four on the front.

While Tammy and Kathryn are whispering at each other, I run over to Britt.

"You entered?"

She smiles. "I can't believe it, but I guess I did."

I look at her rose. "Britt, this is incredible."

Britt shrugs. "I think it's the prettiest one I've ever grown."

"But what about that thing you said—that flowers shouldn't compete with one another and judges are judgy and all that?"

"Oh, I still believe that." Britt nods. "But I also believe that maybe I believe that because I don't quite believe in myself."

"Uhhhh, that's a lot of believing." I raise an eyebrow.

"I guess it was easy for me to sit back and say that contests were stupid, because then I wouldn't have to compete in one. But I've decided that, win or lose, I have to at least try."

"That's really cool of you," I tell her.

"Maybe, but I also just want to beat the smug out of Kathryn and her mother," Britt whispers.

"All entries should be in and ready for judging," the voice over the loudspeaker says. "The judges will be coming around in the next few minutes."

"Hello there, Britt." Dad must have escaped the whispering Woodruffs. "Poppy didn't mention that you'd be here."

"She didn't know," Britt says. "It was a last-minute decision."

Dad looks back at Tammy, and I can see that she's giving him the same glare Kathryn is famous for.

"Well, good luck," he says, and then he meanders back over to Tammy.

Britt stands next to her flower when the judges come by. They take notes in their little notepads, thank Britt, and then move on to the others. I watch as they examine

Kathryn's rose, but their reactions don't change from one flower to the other.

After several minutes, the voice booms over the loudspeaker. "The judges have made their decision."

I squeeze Britt's hand. The judges stand in the front of the display, three ribbons in hand.

"The white ribbon, signifying third place, goes to Gregory Keller," the head judge says, and everybody claps while the judge places the ribbon in front of Gregory's rose.

"The red ribbon, signifying second place," the judge begins, "goes to Kathryn Woodruff!"

I look over at Kathryn, and her face is snow white. She can't even manage a fake smile as the judges present her with the red ribbon. Tammy's face, on the other hand, is a shade of purple I've never seen before.

"And the blue ribbon, signifying first place," the judge says, "goes to Britt Fuller!"

I jump up and down, and throw my arms around Britt.

"You've grown a gorgeous flower, Miss Fuller." The judge places the blue ribbon in front of Britt's vase. "Congratulations."

"Thank you, sir." Britt shakes the judge's hand.

I turn to Kathryn, and tears are rolling down her cheeks. Tammy's talking to her, but her back is to me and

I can't hear what she's saying. Dad is standing on the other side of Tammy, looking like he's trying to disappear.

Tammy grabs Kathryn's hand, and they leave the barn. Dad congratulates Britt, and then reminds me that it's just about time to set up my own project.

"Do you want to wait here for Tammy?" I ask him. "I can get the poster board out of the truck myself."

"I can help," Britt offers.

"No, that's okay, Poppy." Dad pats me on the back. "I'm sure we'll find her later on. She's probably trying to help Kathryn right now."

We walk out of the barn and weave in and out of a sea of people carrying plants, leading horses, and towing bunny pens.

"I know a shortcut." Britt points to the right.

We follow Britt past some smaller outbuildings. It's much easier to walk quickly here, off the beaten path. We pass a small shed when we hear yelling coming from inside.

"I can't believe you let this happen. After all we did to be sure Poppy wouldn't win."

I stop in my tracks, and Britt walks right into me.

Dad's about to say something, but I put my finger to my lips to shush him. Surprisingly enough, he closes his mouth.

"You're crazy, Mom," another voice says. "Poppy was never a threat."

"Maybe not this year. But those roses would have matured and been ready next year. I will not let a Walsh or a Pickler or *anyone* beat us."

I recognize these voices, and by the look on Dad's face, he does too.

"Well, it's too late for that, isn't it?" It's Kathryn. And she's obviously crying. "Because Britt won."

"We could have stopped her," Tammy shrieks. "She's a nothing."

"This is ridiculous, Mom." Kathryn's voice is so quiet I can barely hear it. "They're just flowers."

"I don't know what's wrong with you, Kathryn," Tammy says. "First you let that idiot Thomas almost get you suspended—"

"He didn't tell on me," Kathryn hisses. "I told you he'd cover for me."

"It was too close for comfort. Next year we'll . . ."

"There won't *be* a next year." Kathryn's voice is louder now, more solid. "I'm done with this! You can grow your own flowers, and you can intimidate your own competition. I don't care anymore!"

"Don't you talk to me that way, young lady. We're a team. The Woodruff women!"

"Maybe I don't want to be a team anymore," Kathryn says. "Maybe I just want to have my own life."

And then the shack door swings open, and Kathryn comes running out. She sees us standing there and shakes her head.

"I'm sorry," she croaks, and storms off in the other direction. Tammy comes zipping out after her. She sees us and freezes.

"Oh." Her eyes grow to twice their normal size. "David. I'm sorry. I—It's been a long day and . . . I didn't mean to say that. I—"

Dad puts one arm around my shoulder and one arm around Britt's. "No. I'm glad you did. It's always best to speak the truth. And the truth is, I'd rather not see you again."

And then he steers us toward the parking lot.

CHAPTER 26

I'M INSTRUCTED TO BRING MY PROJECT TO BARN C. I walk in to find a big open space, with tables lining the perimeter of the room. Most of the other displays are already here, so I quickly find an open spot next to a project on global education, and set up. The students are supposed to stand next to their posters, so that anyone who walks by can ask questions.

As soon as my display is up, the barn door opens. A swarm of people come wandering in. I stand next to my poster, giving it a quick once-over. It's not the project I thought I'd have, but I'm proud of it anyway.

"And what do we have here?" An older woman with a pink sweater smiles at me.

"It's a scrapbook," I answer. "Except it's on a poster board instead of in a book."

"Ahhhh." The lady nods. "It's very pretty."

"Thank you." I point to the left side of the poster. "This stuff is from when my mom was my age." There's all the photos that I found in her letters, along with quotes from the letters themselves, the movie stub from *The Breakfast Club*, and the mix tape from Brian. Carefully pinned to the cardboard is the dried rose I found inside *A Popular Guide to Roses*. "And the right side of the poster is about my life." There are photos of Mandy and me, printouts of our texts, the selfie Britt, Brody, and I took while we were planting the roses, some pictures of the baby roses, and the iPod that Brody let me borrow.

"That is fascinating," the woman says. "So many similarities. You even resemble each other. What a fun time you and your mother must have had putting this together."

I look at the picture of Mom with her big hair, and a lump grows in my throat.

The line of people looking at the projects is out the door now. I explain my poster over and over again to each person that comes by, until I recite the lines from memory. I'm grateful for that, because repeating the words over and over again causes them to have less meaning somehow.

After what feels like forever, the line gets shorter, until finally there're just a few people left.

Mrs. Quinn and Mr. Russo are at the end of the line. I straighten my collar and take a sip of water as they approach.

"Hey there, Poppy," Mr. Russo says. "Mrs. Quinn tells me you've got a pretty cool project here."

I smile. "Thank you."

Mr. Russo stops in front of my display and his eyes focus on Mom's side of the poster board. "Well, would you look at that." His voice, usually strong and chipper, is so soft I can barely hear him.

Mrs. Quinn takes her glasses from the chain around her neck and puts them on. She squints at the pictures. "Why, Brian, isn't that you?"

"It sure is." Mr. Russo's eyes are fixed on the photo of Brian and Mom.

Brian and Mom.

Mr. Brian Russo.

Mr. Russo's first name is Brian.

Brian is Mr. Russo!

"I remember when that was taken." Mr. Russo laughs. "We were at the seventh-grade square dance."

"You kids were so cute back then. Hard to believe I taught you all those years ago." Mrs. Quinn winked at me. "I'm older than I look."

I try to speak, but my mouth is so dry, the only thing that comes out of it is a puff of dust.

"Where did you find all this great stuff, Poppy?" Mr. Russo is looking at me. I can only stare back, and that's when I notice that he has the exact same face now as he did then. I can't believe I didn't see it earlier. Sure, his hair is gray, and he's got wrinkles and a beard, but otherwise, it's the same. Same curls. Same kind eyes.

"I . . ." I cough, trying to clear my throat. "I found it. Around the house."

"These are true treasures." He looks back at the photos.

"Mr. Russo," I finally manage to say. "You're Brian? I mean, that's you in the pictures?"

"It sure is." Mr. Russo beams. "I was quite a handsome fellow, wasn't I?" And then he laughs. "In fact, there may be quite a few familiar faces here, Poppy."

Wait. What?

"Let's see . . ." Mr. Russo looks closer at the class photo. "Sure! There's Mike Walker."

"Who?" I squint at the picture.

"Mike Walker. Or, as you know him, Mr. Walker. Your science teacher."

I stare at the photo. "That's Mr. Walker?"

"Indeed," Mr. Russo says.

"And there's Tammy Griffin-Woodruff." Mr. Russo

points to a girl with a high ponytail. I was right. That's Tammy.

"And there's your mom." Mr. Russo gives me a small smile, his eyes looking a little misty. "She was such a sweetheart."

"Yeah, I recognized her immediately." I look at the photo again. Mom's smile is hard to miss.

"Oh, and there's Penelope Topolski, right next to your mother, as usual." Mr. Russo laughs.

"Those two were always inseparable," Mrs. Quinn says.

"I'm sorry. Who?" I had no idea there was someone Mom was inseparable with.

"Right there." Mr. Russo points to a girl right next to Mom. "They were the best of friends."

"Hey!" Mr. Russo snaps his head up, as if he just remembered something very important. "Is that who you were named after?"

"What?" I ask. My mind is spinning.

"Penelope." Mr. Russo points to the girl next to Mom in the photo.

"My name's not Penelope, Mr. Russo. It's Poppy." I'm not sure which one of us is more confused.

"Yes, of course. 'Poppy' was Penelope's nickname all through middle school. We didn't start calling her

Penelope until high school. When we were kids, everyone called her Poppy."

I blink.

"So . . ." I try to talk, but the words get jumbled up in my mouth. I clear my throat and try again. "So my mom's best friend in seventh grade was named Poppy?"

"Sure was." Mr. Russo is still staring at the photo. "Isn't that a hoot?"

CHAPTER 27

"EXCUSE ME," I MUMBLE, AND I RUN OUT OF THE BARN. I need to get some fresh air. I feel like I'm choking.

I walk as fast as I can, even though I have no idea where I'm going. I pass the dairy barn and the poultry barn. I'm about to pass the rabbit pen when I hear someone calling my name.

Britt runs up to me. "Poppy! Wait up."

I stop and look at her, but my mind is somewhere else. "Are you okay?" She's out of breath. "Aren't you supposed to be with your project?"

"Sorry." I put my hands in my hair. "I—I needed some air." And then the tears come. I try to wipe them off my cheeks, but it's no use. They're coming too fast. Just as I'm about to tell Britt the whole story, Brody comes running up to us, a woman wearing a blue zip-up uniform following closely behind.

"Mom?" Britt says when the woman reaches us. "What are you doing here?"

"Brody called me." She's out of breath. "He said you're entering the flower exhibit?"

Britt's ears turn pink. "I am. I did."

"Am I too late? Did they judge already?" Britt's mom looks around, like the flower display will appear in front of her.

"They did judge already." Britt takes the blue ribbon out of her pocket. "I won first place."

"What?" Britt's mom's hands fly to her mouth. "You won?"

Britt nods, and her mom throws her arms around her. "Why didn't you tell me? I would have been here."

"I tried to tell you this morning, but you were running late for work and said you'd talk to me later. Remember?"

"That's what you wanted to say?" Mrs. Fuller shakes her head and squeezes her eyes shut. "What kind of a parent have I been?" But she says it more to herself than to Britt or Brody.

When she opens her eyes, Mrs. Fuller notices that I'm standing there.

"Oh my goodness. I'm so sorry." She looks right at me.

She has the same green eyes as her kids. "How rude of me. I totally interrupted your conversation with Britt."

I wave my hand in front of my face. Actually, the distraction helps. Tears are no longer pouring out of my eyes, so that's a plus. "It's okay, Mrs. Fuller."

"Oh, please call me Penelope."

"Penelope?" I whisper.

"Yes, 'Mrs. Fuller' is my mother-in-law's name. And I never liked that crazy old bat." She laughs.

"Mom, this is our friend Poppy," Britt says. "She's the one who moved into the old Walsh house."

Mrs. Fuller—Penelope—looks like she saw a ghost.

"Poppy? Your name is—oh my goodness. It can't be. Are you . . . You are. You look just like her." Her eyes well up with tears. "You're Daphne's daughter."

"And you're Poppy." Now we're both crying.

"Mom, what are you talking about?" Brody asks.

"I can explain everything," I say, as I wipe my cheek with the back of my hand. I turn to Penelope. "I think I have something that belongs to you."

CHAPTER 28

THE FULLERS FOLLOW ME OVER TO BARN C. IT'S ALMOST empty now, except for a few kids taking down their displays.

When Penelope sees my poster, she gasps.

"Oh my," she says. "Daphne." Tears run down her cheeks.

I pull the last letter out of my pocket and hand it to Penelope. "I think this is supposed to be yours."

She stares at it, and her face melts when she realizes what it is. "This is Daphne's handwriting. I'd recognize it anywhere."

"I found a stack of them in the barn. They're from the spring of 1985."

Penelope holds the letter to her chest. "The spring of

1985. I remember. I went with my parents on a research trip to Greenland."

"Greenland?" I ask.

Penelope nods. "They were scientists, and every year we went to some faraway place. Daphne and I always wrote letters to each other while I was gone. Only in Greenland, I remember, there was no way to get mail."

So that's what Mom meant when she said Poppy was in the "great beyond." She meant Greenland.

"And then, when we got home, your mom went to visit her cousins in New England for the summer. I remember because it was such a boring summer without her. We wrote back and forth while she was there, but I guess those letters that she wrote while I was in Greenland were forgotten about by the time she came home."

"Were you—were you best friends?"

"Oh, honey," Penelope takes my hand. "We were the best of friends. We were practically sisters. We grew up together."

Penelope touches the photo of Mom in the cowboy boots. "After high school, I moved away. I went to college in London, and we just kind of lost touch. By the time I moved back here, she was living in the city, and we just never reconnected. And when I heard she died,

I broke down. It was one of my biggest regrets in life—losing touch with her."

Penelope pulls me into a hug. She smells like mint, and I squeeze my eyes shut.

When I open them, I see Dad walking into the barn. His forehead is wrinkled. He must be wondering why I'm hugging this strange woman.

And then I remember that I told Dad my poster was on plant genetics.

Penelope lets me go, and I smile at Dad. But he's not looking at me. His eyes are fixed to my display.

"Poppy?" Dad glances at me, then his gaze goes back to the poster. "What is this?"

"My project isn't on plant genetics," I say. "Not exactly."

Dad touches the close-up photo of Mom. "Where did you get these?"

"It's a long story," I say. "And I'll tell you everything. I promise. But can we wait until we get home?"

Dad's too mesmerized to answer me.

"Dad?" I touch his arm. "There's someone I'd like you to meet."

Dad blinks and gives me a small smile.

"Dad, this is Penelope Fuller."

Dad extends his hand. "Dave Pickler," he says. He doesn't seem to recognize her name, and then it occurs to me. Maybe he doesn't even know about Penelope.

"It's nice to meet you," Penelope says. "I was—Daphne and I were best friends growing up."

"Penelope? You mean Penelope Topolski?" Dad's eyes instantly well up with tears.

Penelope nods.

"You're Poppy." Dad's mouth falls open, and a flash of recognition crosses his face. "The Poppy our Poppy was named after."

Penelope nods and laughs, and she and Dad fall into a hug. They're both crying and laughing and crying and laughing.

"She talked about you all the time. When we got married, we tried to find you, but in the days before social media it was tough. We had no idea where you were, and your parents had moved away," Dad says.

"I was living overseas," Penelope tells him. "I didn't move back here until I was pregnant with the twins."

"After Daphne passed, I wanted to track you down and tell you." Dad dabs his eye with a finger. "But I couldn't bear the thought of it. Of talking about it. I just couldn't—I just couldn't do anything."

Penelope takes Dad's hands in hers. "I understand. She was so very special."

They look at each other and smile. When I finally turn

to look at Britt and Brody, they're both standing there with their mouths hanging open.

"Mom," Britt says. "You mean the Daphne you always talk about is Poppy's mother?"

Penelope touches Britt's hair. "It appears that way."

"That's crazy," Brody says, shaking his head.

"Why didn't you ever mention Poppy to me?" Penelope asks the twins.

"Are you kidding, Mom?" Britt asks. "I talk about her all the time."

Penelope puts her palms over her eyes. "Oh my goodness. Where have I been?"

"That's a good question," Britt says, barely above a whisper.

"I'm so sorry." Penelope wraps her arms around Britt and Brody. She kisses each of their foreheads, and then her eyes rest on me.

She smiles a sad smile, and I instantly understand.

Mom doesn't care about the 4-H fair. She doesn't care about the blue ribbon. She cares about me. And Dad. And Penelope. She knew we needed to find each other.

CHAPTER 29

DAD, TROY, AND I SIT AT THE KITCHEN TABLE, MY poster board balancing on an empty chair. I tell them about the letters and the pictures, and I even get up the nerve to tell them that I thought the letters were for me. To my surprise, Troy doesn't laugh.

"Sorry that Mom was right about Tammy," I tell Dad. And I really am sorry. He deserves to be happy.

"That's okay, Poppy." Dad touches my cheek. "It just means something better is in store for me."

"I have one important question," Troy says. His lips are pressed together.

"What is it?" Dad's brow is wrinkled, and he looks like he's ready for the inquisition.

"What happened to Mom's hair?" Troy asks.

Dad reaches over and gives him a noogie. "That was the style back then."

Troy shakes his head. "The eighties were so weird."

Dad laughs.

"She had such an awesome smile." Troy's staring at the picture. "I remember one time I was riding my bike, and I fell off. I came into the apartment screaming. She ran to the front door, looking terrified. But as soon as she saw that I only had a scraped knee, she broke into this huge smile. And I knew I'd be all right."

I stare at Troy, wondering if he's being possessed by the ghosts of hillbilly hill. He looks—not sad exactly, more like lost, and then I remember that she was his mom too.

There's a knock on the side door, and I get up to answer it. Britt, Brody, and Penelope walk into the mudroom.

"I hope this is an okay time," Penelope says.

"Yes, of course." I step aside. "Come in."

"Actually," Penelope says, "we were hoping you'd come out. We'd like to take you somewhere."

I yell for Dad and Troy. Dad walks into the mudroom, and his face lights up when he sees Penelope.

"We're wondering if you wouldn't mind taking a ride with us," Penelope says. "We have a surprise."

"Sure," Dad says, "I'll get the car keys."

"We can all fit in my car, if that's okay with you?"

"You bet," Dad says, and we follow the Fullers out into the driveway. We all pile into their SUV, and Penelope rolls down the windows. The warm air blows my hair back, and I turn to Britt and Brody, smiling.

"Where are we going?" I whisper.

"It's a surprise," Brody whispers back.

After a few minutes, we pull into the cemetery where Mom, Grandad, and Grandmom are buried. Penelope's car slowly approaches Mom's grave site.

We all get out of the car.

"I have something for you," Britt says. She pulls a box out of the back. Inside is a perfect, potted rosebush.

"Oh, Britt," I say. "It's gorgeous."

Brody grabs a shovel and some gloves, and starts digging a hole in front of Mom's headstone.

"No." I touch his hand. "Let me."

Brody hands me the shovel, and I finish digging. Britt gives the rosebush to Dad, and he places it gently into the hole. As Troy packs the soil around the bush, Penelope pulls a bag of mulch out of the car. She sprinkles mulch on top of the soil and then pats it down with her hands.

"She'll love it," I say.

We stand at the grave site in silence for several minutes. It feels good to be here all together. I'm sure it's what Mom wanted all along.

"One more thing," Penelope says, and she pulls the envelope I gave her earlier out of her pocket. She rips it open and reads Mom's letter out loud.

June 1, 1985

Dear Poppy,

The fair was today. I came in second. Guess who came in first? Tammy, of course. I know I should be more upset than I am, but the truth is, I'm still proud. Second out of almost fifty entries is pretty good.

Plus, Brian held my hand today as we walked through the fair. Is there anything better than that?

As a matter of fact . . . there is! The best news ever is that you come home from the Great Beyond next week! Sure, we'll only have a couple of weeks together until I go to my cousins in Boston, but still . . . two weeks of fun and catching up! These last couple of months have just reminded me of how important our friendship is, Poppy, and I hope we're never apart again.

Until next week (when I see you in person!!!!).

Love & friendship always & forever,
Daphne

I look up, and everybody's teary-eyed. Even Troy, although he's trying to hide it by lowering his baseball hat over his eyes.

Penelope takes my hand. I take Brody's. Brody takes Britt's. Britt takes Troy's. Troy takes Dad's, and Dad takes Penelope's, until the circle is complete.

We stand there in silence for a long time, each linked together through Mom's love.

"Who's hungry?" Dad finally asks. "I have some fresh veggies back at the house. We can whip together some salad and sandwiches."

"That sounds wonderful," Penelope says.

We spend the car ride back laughing and talking. Penelope pulls up to the garage, and everyone pours out of the car. We pass the garden as we enter the house, and that's when we see it.

I don't have to look around to know that every single one of us is frozen, unable to move.

Because my garden is covered with flowers.

And not just any flowers.

My garden is covered with poppies.

"How—" Penelope starts to say.

"I don't understand," I say. And then I turn to Britt. "When you gave us those rose seeds, are you sure they were rose seeds?"

"Of course." Britt can't keep her eyes off the garden. "Rose seeds and poppy seeds look nothing alike."

I remember the seeds we planted. They looked like pebbles. And the only poppy seeds I've seen are the ones on a bagel. They're tiny and black, and look nothing like the seeds we planted in the garden that day.

"So how . . . how did these get here?" Brody asks.

"There must have been a mistake," Dad says. "You must have had the wrong seeds."

But as he says it, I know even he doesn't believe his own words.

Mom always wanted us to have roots somewhere. And before we could have roots, we needed to have seeds.

And now we have both.

ACKNOWLEDGMENTS

Thank you to my wonderful editor, Alyson Heller. It is truly a pleasure to work with you! Thanks for believing in my vision and for cheering Poppy on all the way. Thanks also to everyone at Simon & Schuster who brought Poppy's story to life. Your behind-the-scenes work is greatly appreciated.

A big thank-you to my agent, the brilliant Sarah Davies, for your unwavering support and faith in me. I'm looking forward to many more books together!

Thank you to cover artist Stevie Lewis for capturing Poppy's connection to her mother (and her trip through the 80s) so beautifully.

As always, a squishy group hug to the MGBetaReaders, the most creative, smartest, and funniest critique group I could ever ask for. Special thanks to Poppy's early readers Jen Malone and Brooks Benjamin. I'm blessed to call you my friends.

To all my middle school and high school friends, I'm so glad I saved the notes we wrote! I'm brought back in time whenever I open that old box, and I feel a little sad that my own kids won't have that experience of putting pen to paper and discreetly passing those folded-up gems in the hallway between classes.

Thank you to my parents, who taught me that magic always follows if you do the work. It's a lesson I hope to teach my own children. Hear that, Hallie and Morgan? You can get anything you dream of . . . as long as you're willing to work for it. And while I have your attention, thank you for reading, thank you for commenting, thank you for just being you. I'm so grateful to be your mom. Thanks to Josh, for reading far below your grade level and well out of your genre. Your input is greatly appreciated! And thanks for handling the dinner, laundry, dishes (I could go on and on) when I'm engrossed in my own little writing world.

And finally, a huge thanks to you, the reader! I'm so happy that you chose to spend your time with Poppy and friends!